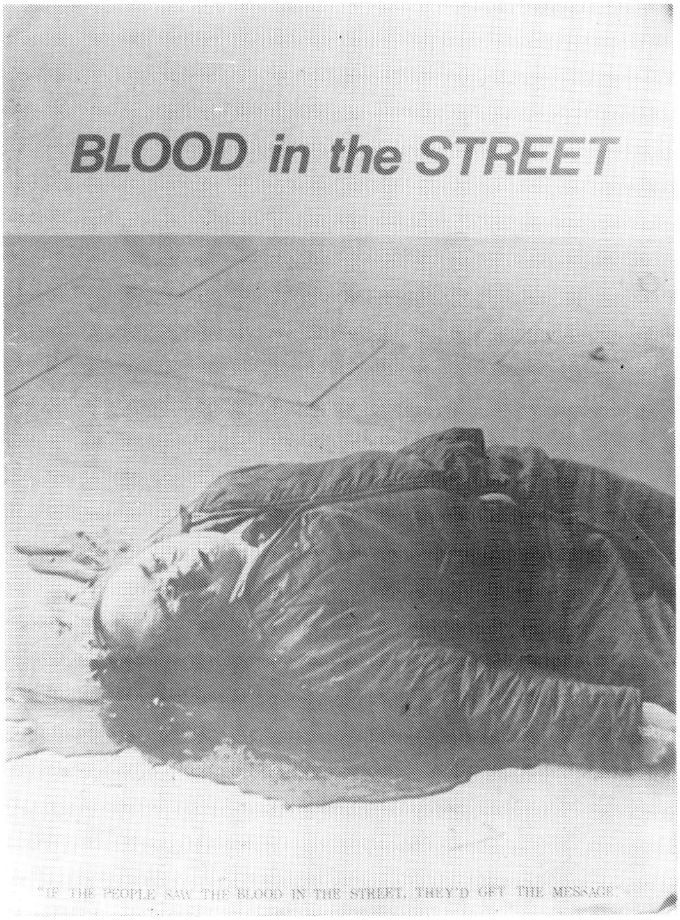
BLOOD in the STREET
"IF THE PEOPLE SAW THE BLOOD IN THE STREET, THEY'D GET THE MESSAGE"

First published in March 1972 by
Peoples' Democracy and Lotta Continua

This edition published in October 1998 by
Guildhall Press, 41 Great James Street
Derry, Northern Ireland BT48 7DF
Tel: (01504) 364413 Fax: (01504) 372949
E-mail: gpress@compuserve.com

Cover photograph courtesy of the *Derry Journal*

Printed in Northern Ireland by Coleraine Printing Company

ISBN 0 946451 50 8

Guildhall Press receives support from the Training & Employment Agency under the Action for Community Employment scheme. Special thanks to Manus Martin (T&EA), and Derry City Council's Recreation and Leisure Department for generous Community Services Grant Aid.

Editorial Note

Blood in the Street was first published in March 1972, prior to the publication of the Widgery Report. Most of the text, ie Grimaldi and North's account of the events of Sunday 30 January 1972, was written in the days immediately following Bloody Sunday, much of it directly transcribed from tapes made on the day itself. The taped conversations recorded in the homes of some of the victims and with some of those injured and still in hospital took place within two to three weeks of Bloody Sunday. Only 2-300 copies were produced in the English language (a similar amount were produced in Italian), making it one of the rarest publications on the Northern Irish conflict.

In producing this reprint we have tried to duplicate the original, beginning on page 10, as closely as possible, staying with the original design and layout, and only correcting any spelling mistakes. The front cover, reproduced on the title page, has been changed at the request of the family of the late Bernard McGuigan. The original back cover image, a photograph of Free Derry Corner, and the now out of date contact addresses on the inside back cover, have been omitted. Many of the original negatives were unavailable at the time of going to print, so copies had to be made from the original publication, hence the poor quality of some of the photographs contained within the book.

Guildhall Press would like to extend our thanks to the Bloody Sunday Justice Campaign and the Bloody Sunday Trust for their support for this publication, to Fulvio Grimaldi for allowing us to reproduce his work and for providing a new preface for the book, Don Mullan for writing the introduction, the Bogside Artists for the inspiration for the cover design, and to June McCloskey and Sean O'Doherty, without whose foresight in preserving original copies of *Blood in the Street* this reprint would have been impossible.

Adrian Kerr
October 1998

INCUBATORS OF VIOLENCE

An Introduction to *BLOOD in the STREET*
by Don Mullan

BLOODY SUNDAY – SOUNDS AND SCENES

An anonymous Derry boy, shortly after the massacre of Bloody Sunday said, "I am glad that people like you exist". The compliment was spoken to, and about, Italian photo-journalist Fulvio Grimaldi.

Grimaldi had come to Derry with his English born partner, Susan North, to record the sounds and scenes of a Northern Ireland civil rights march to be held in Derry on Sunday 30 January 1972. By then, civil rights demonstrations were common occurrences and the fact that this one had been banned, wasn't particularly out of the ordinary. What occurred, however, shocked Grimaldi and North to the core and propelled them to counteract the malevolent untruths about Bloody Sunday which the British establishment were successfully choreographing around the world.

We should not lose sight of the fact that the first edition of this book was published in March 1972 with Grimaldi's narrative written within days of Bloody Sunday. It is obvious the first edition was prepared hastily, lacking perhaps the finesse which might otherwise have characterised a publication which was not motivated by a prophetic sense of urgency to tell the truth and to defy the barefaced lying on the part of powerful British Institutions of State.

It should be remembered that Fulvio Grimaldi and Susan North risked their lives in the common service of humanity that day. Grimaldi, in fact, could easily have been the 15th victim of Bloody Sunday and his name might well have adorned the Rossville Street memorial, if the Para's had their way. Amongst the many crimes committed by the 1st Battalion the Parachute Regiment on that day, against a civilian population, it must never be forgotten that they attempted to murder an Italian photographer on at least two occasions. A photo-journalist who was simply doing his job of recording history and the truth.

WE BELONGED

Those of us who survived the chilling terror of those 30 minutes of military madness can easily identify with the surreal language which Grimaldi uses throughout his text. There is a poetic quality woven throughout by a man who, along with his partner and the people of Derry, confronted and defied death on several occasions and, in the process, became as one:

> "...bang-kchhhh, bang-kchhhh, against real human beings. The scream hit louder than all the explosions. It hit and stunned. It's live. And suddenly we were faced with death. It wasn't a question of sores, bruises, lung congestion, freezing water any more. It was death or life. The absolute alternative. For everybody. Those with camera and press card included. As never before, more than political and human affinity and solidarity had ever achieved, we, observers, reporters, uninvolved parties, were part of the one side, the

people's side. And we accepted the identification, automatically, naturally. The mechanism of death was after us too, ready to catch up, grind, obliterate. The alternative of running in the opposite direction, away from the people who had to be killed. Behind the barriers of safety and officialdom, of 'impartiality', didn't even cross our minds. And it certainly wasn't because [on] this side of the fence better professional opportunities were offered, the prospect of some unique scoop, recognition, popularity, money. The message that those live bullets carried directly to you, did away with that. It was just that we felt, without thinking, without rationalising, that we belonged to the running and screaming and falling and dying and hating and despairing: the people, and not the ludicrous little death-spitters that invisible strings made hop around and chase and shoot and kill. As simple as that..."

DEATH FROM THE WALLS

Grimaldi and North, it should be remembered too, were amongst the first to suspect that some of the Bloody Sunday dead had been shot from the Derry Walls. And this, back in 1972! On page 37, one of their headings reads: "Target Practice. Death from the Walls". Their interview with 32 year old Daniel McGowan in Altnagelvin Hospital, clearly records his suspicion that he had been wounded from on high: "I think the shot came from the Walls. The position I was in, the bullet went in the left side of my leg, came out at my foot, the right side. There was no Saracen. It must have come from Derry Walls..." McGowan was shot at the bottom of the steps which ran from the Rossville Flats forecourt up to Fahan Street.

In this context there is also an extraordinary interview with Alexander Nash, himself wounded as he tried to recover the body of his son William from the Rossville Street barricade. William we now suspect was shot dead on Bloody Sunday by a hidden marksman operating in the vicinity of the Derry Walls, alongside John Young and Michael McDaid. Alexander Nash and his family only discovered this as the 25th anniversary of William's death approached. But Grimaldi records Alexander Nash saying the following:

> "We don't know who's doing this shooting from the Walls. You don't know it. Another dead. Them boys are being let loose with the rifles. We don't know who is doing the shooting from the Walls..."

The Lord Chief Justice of England, Lord Widgery, if he possessed the integrity his high office demanded, had the powers to discover the full truth about how, why and from where, all of the Bloody Sunday dead and wounded were shot. As Grimaldi, North and Daniel McGowan demonstrate, there was enough suspicion and evidence to warrant investigation. The fact that Widgery choose to ignore this evidence serves only to increase our suspicions that the Walls might yet prove to be the British Establishment's Achilles heel. It is not the presence of a hidden marksman, I suspect, which Widgery wished to hide, but rather that of very senior military personnel (and perhaps others), which would lend weight to our belief that Bloody Sunday was a politically sanctioned massacre.

THROBBING DETAILS

Grimaldi's narrative is awash with throbbing details and insights which, at times, leave the reader breathless. One can sense the eye of an artist surveying an unfolding nightmare with deepening despair and foreboding.

> "A helmet shone under the sun and caught my eye. The area in front of me was getting deserted. The glimmer on the helmet bounced up and down as its owner ran after a tiny, unreal group...
>
> The Saracen is there. Heavy and still, like a big beast after its meal...
>
> ...more Saracens were moving in, with soldiers flanking and following on foot, guns at the ready. Germans mopping up some Warsaw ghetto, I reflected. And as I hurried up the street, the glimpse of childhood fantasy shot through my mind: when walking along narrow alleys, I imagined some huge ice-breaking vessel moving up the road, with steel pushers wiping away whatever they met on the way and I tried to figure some way of getting away, flying up perhaps, and ended up with images of smashed flesh, of bones crunched against the walls flanking the street, and dreaded the thought that this ice-breaker should ever come true. There it was, slowly and horribly moving up the street, determined to crush anything. Come true.
>
> The man who shouted crumbles to a heap and slowly stretches out. Like the gradual deflating of a balloon."

Grimaldi's ever growing outrage and revulsion at what he is witnessing finds expression in a mocking disdain for the Paratroopers whom he describes throughout as "spitting insects".

> "The soulless mechanical tools. And their masters, the mad, frothing, mad scientists.
>
> I keep remembering the paratroopers as tiny, artificial, mechanical, and the people as normal sized, or even larger than life.
>
> Paratroopers. The helmet, round and bulky like a casserole...
>
> ...first aid men and girls among them, red eyes, tears in their eyes, working professionally, pedantically, not giving a damn about themselves. The bravest people in the world. In front and under the guns, under the narrow, masked gaze of insects, the greatest cowards in the world."

CURSE OF THE DEAD GENERATIONS

This small volume is a treasure chest of aching memories written and compiled by an Italian and an English journalist who are unapologetic about their partisan and passionate crusade. In many respects Grimaldi and North provide an essential insight into the mountain of hurt and humiliation, compounded by decades of official acquiescence and state sanctioned terrorism, which helped spawn and strengthen a generation of urban guerrillas whose discipline, deathly determination and defiance shocked and sometimes horrified even their own communities. This perhaps is best illustrated in Grimaldi's recording of a deeply traumatised mother who invokes the curses of dead generations on the paratroopers and their masters:

> "Tell the world, tell about the murderers... We shall not surrender... The curse of the dead generations on the murderers... and all the generations to come. They won't get us, never. And they will not beat us..."

Grimaldi reflects on the impact of the paratroopers actions and the official cover-up. Actions which were to exacerbate the consequences of that day for quarter of a century to follow. His words are indeed prophetic:

> "And one can see why these things produce IRA, victory. Because they produce togetherness, closeness, understanding of who and what the enemy really is, force. They feed the monster for minutes, hours, days perhaps. But they make togetherness, Sinn Féin, IRA, Revolution, for ever."

Grimaldi also records the gentler side of Derry life which was, and remains, part and partial of a unique community spirit. Amidst the growing anguish of that day, the mother of the murdered Jim Wray takes pity on a young shivering woman who was soaked by a water cannon. She invites her back to the Wray family home in the Bogside to let her have a warm bath and to find her a change of clothing. Later, when she had discovered the horrific circumstances of her son's death (Jim was shot in the back as he lay already wounded in Glenfada Park), and in spite of her pain and unfathomable sorrow, Mrs Wray told Grimaldi:

> "They let my son die like a dog in the street, and if a paratrooper was laying there now, I would go to him and see could I do somethin' for him, and I would bring his clergy to give him the last rites of his church."

POLITICAL OVERTONES

The cold and calculated nature of Bloody Sunday makes it very difficult to conclude that what happened on the day was the result of a small band of soldiers losing control or mistaking incoming fire from the Derry Walls as an IRA attack. The presence in Derry of General Ford, the commander of British Army land forces in Northern Ireland, of 1800 troops and eight regiments, all of whom were engaged in sealing off the no-go areas of Creggan, Brandywell and the Bogside, form a pattern which suggests that an unprecedented military operation was in progress. When this is coupled with the genuine forewarnings given by some British military personnel to local girlfriends, and others, to stay away from the civil rights march because something dreadful was going to happen, we are left with no other conclusion than Bloody Sunday was a planned massacre with strong political overtones.

Was, for example, Bloody Sunday part of a last gasp effort by the old Stormont regime to kill the Northern Ireland Civil Rights Movement and to so traumatise the Nationalist community in general whereby it would be beaten back into submissiveness for a few more generations? I believe it was. Quite the opposite, of course, happened. The resulting decades of brutal political and sectarian violence owes much to what British Paratroopers did in Derry that day and the labyrinth of official lies which a British Prime Minister, a British Parliament and a British Lord Chief Justice concocted to cover-up the horror of those actions.

NEW BLOODY SUNDAY INQUIRY

With the establishment of the new Bloody Sunday Inquiry, the British Government has the opportunity to put right great wrongs of historic proportions. Lord Saville of Newdigate, Chairman of the new Inquiry, and his two Commonwealth panellists, Sir Edward Somers, New Zealand, and Mr Justice Hoyt, Canada, have assumed an enormous responsibility. They cannot presume the confidence of the families who lost their loved ones, the Bloody Sunday wounded, or the wider Nationalist community of Derry and beyond. Lord Chief Justice Widgery has cast a long shadow of suspicion and our engagement with the new inquiry will always be in the knowledge that their predecessor caused enormous distress and hurt through the abuse of the same powers they now possess. Saville, Somers and Hoyt might yet contribute to the healing process so necessary between the peoples of Ireland and their British neighbours, if on this occasion they apply themselves to the fair and impartial unravelling of the truth which they promised in their opening statement on 3 April 1998.

An essential part of that truth is a recognition of the primary source of the political violence which has so characterised the unresolved consequences of British colonialism on this part of the island, better known as 'Northern Ireland'. Grimaldi's photographs, narrative and the sound recordings he made with Susan North, help to bring into sharp relief one abiding truth which I personally know from my upbringing amongst the good people of the Creggan, Brandywell and Bogside: *The community into which I was born was not itself conceived with a genetic defect that made it prone to violence.*

How and why a peace loving community (which I come from), can begin to produce and support a deadly and disciplined guerrilla army, demands greater honesty and accountability from politicians and lawmakers. Centuries of colonial abuse and decades of political corruption are surely the incubators which breed the despicable virus of violence.

Don Mullan
Derry, 1 October 1998

Preface

Thank you, 1st Battalion Paras. Thank you. Much of what helped me detect, in my human and professional experiences, the difference between right and wrong, justice and injustice, valour and cowardice, love and contempt, slavery and freedom, I owe to you, 1st Battalion.

Almost 27 years have gone since what was to become the most important event in my professional, political, social and ethical life. Whenever, upon coming to write or speak about a news item, I happened to be in doubt over who should be supported and who criticised or condemned, the Bloody Sunday experience, the faces on one side and those on the other, helped me take my decision. If I managed to remain an honest journalist, ever biased in favour of the oppressed, this I owe you, 1st Battalion.

You showed me with utmost precision and efficiency what lurks behind power, wealth, self-righteousness, conceit, officialdom, media-obedience. You showed me violence and death, fraud and dishonesty and, in contrast, the dead, or dying or suffering faces of the working (or more likely unemployed) people of Derry offered me a flower whose petals I remember as courage, sincerity, liberty, solidarity, love, life. This flower I have never stopped watering. Its blossoms are as strong and as beautiful as ever. May they shine over our precarious future.

Fulvio Grimaldi
Rome, 28 September 1998

dedicated
to the ordinary people
of Free Derry
to their suffering
their courage
their struggle
their victory
their Freedom

Foreword by the authors

What Hitler, by Capital and Business created and supported, did to Jews, Czechoslovakians, Italians, Poles, French, Soviets, Greeks and many other nationalities, and to his own working people, the British ruling class, as led by the City and represented by British Governments, are doing to the national and working class population of Northern Ireland. Concentration camps, torture, murder, suppression of political liberties and human rights included. Plus neocapitalistic forms of exploitation and economical blackmail.

In the planned and efficiently executed genocide of the Irish national working class in the North, the British enjoy the complicity and the encouragement of Northern Irish fascist puppet governments, representing the local ruling class whose survival as holders of the power and wealth monopoly can only be guaranteed by continued exploitation and oppression, and today, as the ordinary people of Northern Ireland have taken to armed revolution, by total coercion through the means of the British Army.

The mass murder of the Derry poor, which we had the extraordinary luck and unmeasurable grief to witness from the side upon which it has been inflicted, is the culmination of a design intended to break the revolutionary national and social struggle, and to pave the way for deceitful "reforms" that the people, and their advanced level of struggle, would have never accepted and would have fought as long as armed with the one power that oppressors respect, understand and fear - the gun.

But the slaughter of the Derry poor, in the moment of their defencelessness, is also something else. It is the paranoiac reaction of a schizophrenic society in its final convulsions, feeling the death sting of total challenge and of total rejection. Challenge and rejection by 40,000 working class people during three years of freedom and resistance.

Offensive Resistance, that has made exploiting and oppressing minorities shudder with terror, from Belfast to London, from Dublin to Bonn, from Paris to Rome, from Moscow to Washington, from Saigon to Tokyo, from Madrid to Athens, from Ankara to Rio de Janeiro. Offensive Resistance, the infectious power of which is encouraging and strengthening the efforts and determination and hopes of the oppressed, exploited, persecuted majority of the human race throughout the world. Free Derry is the guiding light of the marching have-nots.

It will be said that this book about the State-butchery in Derry is one-sided and partial. That it is emotional. We, who have written it, and the people about whom it is and the people for whom it is, don't mind and don't care. Our emotions are criticised and feared because they carry us to victory. Our partiality and one-sidedness is indicted because it reflects the part and the side of us, the masses, the people. We are not interested in objectivity, aloofness, that can only derive from indifference or vested complicity with those who have everything to lose.

We have nothing to lose but the truth. We have everything to gain. This is our strength, our invincible strength.

We apologise if the imperfect knowledge of English of who wrote down the story of Bloody Sunday will cause difficulties to the reading friends. We hope in their indulgence, considering that this account may well be seen as the loving contribution of the friends of Free Derry in all the world.

DUBLIN — Fulvio Grimaldi

ROME — Susan North

LONDON February 1972

INTRODUCTION

by Peter McMullan

who deserted from the Parachute Regiment

three days before Bloody Sunday

after nine years of service

in the British Army

and after having blown up

with three bombs

Palace Barracks, Holywood, Belfast.

It started when I was fifteen. I wanted to be a chef and when I took a job in Belfast the wages were so poor that the army was the only place where I could get a good training plus a good wage. I worked in Belfast for about three months, with earnings at nineteen shillings a week and then, when I went to the Army, my wages rose to the region of somewhere around five pounds a week, while I was being trained, plus food and clothing and everything else, which wasn't provided in the job I had in Belfast.

I had to sign on for nine years, which excluded my training period of three years. In other words, twelve years altogether, with no way out. After I had been fully trained there was no way out. I couldn't buy myself out or anything like that. I had to do the full twelve years.

I went to Aldershot, where all cooks in the Army go to be trained. It's the biggest school in the world and I was part of the Army Catering College. I have done the initial six weeks of square bashing, rifle training, learning how to march, learn how to act as a body of men, as the army put it, weaponry, you know, field exercises, concealment.

When I became a paratrooper the training was different all together. This was the normal training that every soldier does in the army, intermingled with the regimental history and a little bit of education. No political education whatsoever. Propaganda-wise, as far as the Army or the history of the Regiment was concerned, yes, lots. They always told you the feats and the greatness of the Regiment, how many battle honours it had won or how many great battles it had been involved in. No outlook into the outside world, none at all in fact. The first three months of my Army career I was out of the barracks twice to take part in civilian life, you know.

The Army was run as a boarding school, except the discipline was much more rigid. You would be punished the same way as a regular soldier, they could put you in jail or take money off you in fines, or you could lose your rank if you had any, the hardest tasks to do, scrubbing barracks or working in the cooking house. For very very little, if you were cheeky to a senior soldier, if they told you to do something and you said you'd do it in a minute or something like that. For very very little they could have you, that could lose you a fiver, or you could be made to work in the cook house for two hours every night, and make the parade four times a day in all your best uniform, which was far worse.

In 1968 I joined the Paratroop Regiment as an ordinary soldier. This was an entirely different organisation. To start off with, I was sent to Aldershot again, which is the home of the Paratroop Regiment. I had a ten days selection course in which I was required to pass certain physical tests, an educational test and a coordination test. When I completed these I went for a personal interview with an officer of the Regiment and on the reports from all the tests that I'd done and his recommendation I was put forward again for another eight week test, to be selected.

Among the tests there was a confidence course, which consisted of very very high scaffolding with a nine inch plank on top of it, and you had to run along it, with various obstacles on it. It was dangerous. Anybody could have slipped, fallen, I mean, you were thirty, forty feet up in the air with nothing, no safety nets or anything. This was your confidence test, you know. There was another one, scaffolding, pure scaffolding, with a net hanging on the outside of the scaffolding, about eighty feet high. And on the top of this, again, there was one piece of scaffolding, piping. You had to climb onto this and walk across it. When you got to the middle of it you bent down and touched your toes and then went straight up and put your hands as high in the air as possible and shout your name. The idea of shouting your name was to make you lose balance, 'cause your mind is taken off your balance. There was one chap, he fell off the 40 foot scaffolding. He broke his bones.

The Regimental history, again, in the Parachute regiment, is very very much drummed into you: the great war victories and feats since 1942, when they were formed. They have 36 battle honours. Training is very very hard, harder than the Marine Commandos. Physical fitness is their biggest thing. Also an awareness to the Regimental History and the propaganda of the Regiment. In other words, when you put on a red beret you are the greatest. Nobody can beat you. The second thing is an awareness to the orders: you must always jump to the orders.

At the end of the sixteenth week you and whoever is left of the selection go against all other soldiers in the British Army who want to be Parachutists and you are set up in a number of eight tests and you compete in these eight tests. Two very very long runs with kit, under timing, ten miles in 65 minutes.

Accidents are frequent. On the ranges in my time, there was one person shot by live ammunition. Previous to that there had been about four men killed using live ammunition. 95 per cent of your training is done under live ammunition fire, and they fire on cross fire at the men who are doing an attack on the house, or skirmishing or doing a raid. All fire directed at you. Also one pound charges of explosives are used, which are let go off anywhere around you. A person sits about three hundred yards away and pulls little switches and off go the explosives all around you. I myself had three accidents. You see, I have no knuckle there. That was done in a fight. When they put you in a ring with another man you just fight it out, to find out just how aggressive you are, you know. I have known boots and heads being used, and people biting and kneeing people. In the heat of the fight this can go on, you know. I have seen people badly injured from that. I was badly injured from it. Another time, at somersaults, I pulled all ligaments in my leg. The assault course the paras do, which is very strenuous and hard, is all done in water and because of the cold it was all iced up. Well, one of the chaps fell about fifteen feet and landed on his head, on the ice. That chap lost his memory and has been having headaches ever since. These type of injuries happen fairly often. Parachuting accidents are the worst: people jumping out and landing wrongly or parachutes fail to open, broken legs, people getting killed. Possibly twelve men a year lose their lives through parachuting, you know. I would say more. Last year there was twenty four killed.

The people who join the paras? People who like adventure, who don't like to be in the same place all the time, above all people who are naturally aggressive anyway, because you have to be naturally aggressive to join the Parachute Regiment. There has to be a streak of viciousness in you, I'd say. They are mostly labourers, farm-workers, people like that, fairly poor...

Abuse. It's fairly hard for most men to take, because you live the life of a dog while you are in training, because they can do anything they want to you, they can beat you up, they can kick you, they can swear at you, they can call you whatever they like. They can make fun of your family, they can make fun of you, they can make fun of your wife. And they do.

The punishments. In a Parachute Regiment jail the life is all centred on physical work. In the morning you run up to seventeen miles. After breakfast you go out and you work with the log, running with the log, which is a telegraph pole, fairly heavy. On one occasion prisoners taken in from another Regiment didn't like the treatment and mutinied and they locked themselves in the cells. They couldn't take any more of it.

The officers get political education, as regards the different countries, Vietnam, Ireland when it came up, Sarawak, anywhere there is a conflict. Before I came to Ireland myself, we had a political exercise which gave the different aspects of the political set up in Northern Ireland. This was just after the Burntollet affair. Of the Civil Rights they said that they were all communists, Michael Farrel, McCann, Devlin. What it really boiled down to: the CRA was a communist movement, which the IRA had infiltrated. There was no question about it being a two-sided conflict. Everything was centred upon the Civil Rights as being militants, communists, law breakers, hooligans, what have you. Like cowboys and Indians.

While I was in training we were shown films of Russians indoctrinating Westerners. Interrogation films, you know. Their brain washing methods. These were the techniques that we were shown. They were worked on us by SAS and military police. That was communism. Literature was restricted. You could have the odd magazine with ladies. Subversive literature, a book written on the IRA or on Che Guevara, was definitely out. If you were caught with it, you took the consequences. They weren't allowed.

Social life. Getting out and getting drunk and fighting, this type of having a good time. Personally I don't agree with it, I had a family, I was married when I was seventeen, most of my life was centred around the family. The officers approve of this kind of social life. Again, it's their aggressive play, you know. They think it's good if men can have a good punch up, maim and injure other people.

The paratroopers look down their noses on the other soldiers. They are always on the top, they think. The same as regards the civilians. This time last year three paratroopers left a young man, in Aldershot, laying on the roadside after having kicked him half to death. They have no regard for this type of human life. When they go into a fight they show their aggressiveness to the fullest extent, you know. They are brutal in every aspect.

Coloured people are just not accepted into the Parachute Regiment. They use every conceivable way of keeping them out. Since I was in it there was only one coloured boy and to this day there is only two in my battalion. They are just not accepted. They have to be exceptional persons to be accepted. And even though they are accepted, they are still frowned upon and looked upon as the black nigger and they take the abuse and they have to take it to stay with it.

A number of men have cracked up. The last time we were in Belfast, two in particular. One who had been in the Albert Street Mill took his rifle, went up on the top of the mill and started shooting at the soldiers below. This man was quietened down and he is now in a mental hospital. Another chap, who was a friend of mine actually, he took his weapon out one night and he threatened to shoot his platoon sergeant. Again he was talked out of it and went into a mental home. Now he has a job as a clerk. They have a high number of people who have cracked up under the mental strain, you know. People will just drop by the wayside, during running, and just totally refuse to go on any more. And no matter how much they kick them and beat them, they just won't go up.

I was in Cyprus, Germany, Aden, Malta, Canada, America, Bahrein, Turkey... In Cyprus there was big animosity towards the Greeks. The Turkish people, we were allowed to go along with them. On the Greeks it was very very hard. Lots of fights, lots of punch-ups, lots of people injured. In Aden, during the troubles, there was almost a Bloody Sunday every week, the killings you know, people were killed, children. They didn't really have any respect for the people, they were Arabs, they were pigs, wogs, you know. If you were an Arab or a Greek, you were just a wog. That's just their attitude: you're a wog. No respect at all for them. No fraternisation in Aden. There was always the odd prostitute, you know. That wasn't minded. That is your aggressive sort of playtime. It's a bachelors life, you know, although, I would say, about seventy percent of them are married.

First time I came to Northern Ireland was in 1969. This was a four month active service tour, which started on the night of the 15th of August, the bad shooting. The first time soldiers were shot at. On the Shankill Road. Forty men of the King's Regiment were shot. The King's Regiment was taken off and Faulkner sent the Paratroopers on. It was the Cup-of-tea-Brigade. You had the cups of tea from everybody and the cream buns, you know. At the same time you were expected to get as much information as regards weapons and any military equipment that was hidden on the Shankill Road and at the time they knew it was hidden on the Shankill Road. A couple of raids would have done it. While I was on the Shankill road I was briefed three times on the amount of ammunition and guns on the Shankill Road. In the words of Colonel Mike Gray, our O.C., there was enough guns to equip his Parachute Battalion, 750 men, you know.

He used to go and have little meetings every Friday night with McQuade, M.P., who was involved in the Malvern Street murder of 1966. He was the head of the Civil Defence Committee on the Shankill Road. During the time on the Shankill Road I didn't really see any impartiality at all. In fact it was more partial than impartial. One night in a pub, I had an argument with a fella because I disagreed entirely about what he was saying about the Catholic population of the country. Myself being a Catholic, my family living in the North of Ireland, my wife's family living there, seeing the suffering of other people in the North of Ireland, seeing 32 houses burnt in Coches Street while the British soldiers stood there with their rifles and watched Protestants burning the houses and not doing nothing about it. I didn't think the Army was very impartial. So I asked to be removed from the streets of Belfast as I said I wouldn't fight whilst the army took this line of "peace keeping" as they said. My brother's house was shot at by the Protestants, the houses in Coches Street were burnt, a few other things happened and when I put this to Colonel Gray he said that I personally wouldn't be impartial. I explained to him that he was having his cups of tea every night with Mr. McQuade, his bingo sessions with Mr. McQuade, that he was never going over to the Falls Road to have cups of tea with the leaders over there...

Before I came over here, you could have said possibly that I was anti-Irish. I hadn't been brought up in Ireland, I had only lived there a year and a half. It didn't really interest me at all, until I had seen, you know, the injustices being meted out. Then I realised what was right and what was wrong. Historical background and present life in Ireland, I didn't know an awful lot about, at all. I knew jobs was hard to come by for certain people, my father had trouble in getting a job because of his religion, but I didn't think it was so widespread, you know. It took me to see exactly what was going on, to find out how I would take a stand myself. The Army had always put it across that the Civil Rights was wrong and everyone else was right. The other soldiers only saw their own officers going to the minister's clubs, to people like John McQuade. They gave me the impression that they weren't really interested. If the officers thought that these particular people were right, they would also follow in their thinking. There was one particular person I remember well. He joined the Army with me and had been in the same platoon. He was the only man I'd ever seen to stand up and give his own point of view. He was severely rebuked. He had gone up and had said that the Catholics had been definitely oppressed, the job situation was definitely not in their favour, and the housing, and normal life. This person was told to shut up.

The fact is that the Army weren't particularly interested in who was right and who was wrong. Although they were one-sided and were going further to the one side all the time. They had clubs on the Shankill Road, they had no clubs on the Falls Road. They had parties for children on the Shankill Road, they had no parties for children on the Falls road. They had dances on the Shankill, they opened a dance hall in Coches Street, and nothing on the other side.

The IRA for the Army? Subversives, murderers, they didn't even term them as guerrillas, you know. They weren't freedom fighters as far as anybody was concerned. They didn't even see the point in questioning their motivations. Although a whole lot of them said why should we be in Northern Ireland? Why should we give them all this money - in their terms - to keep this damned country going? They weren't really interested in being here. It was just another job, you know, another dreary job. Because the conditions when we first went to Northern Ireland were very very bad for the soldiers. I used to go on patrol and if it rained and I was wet, well then I had to go into a sleeping bag. And when I woke the next morning I was still wet. Well, I beg your pardon, you'd do two hours on and you had two hours off. Although you got plenty of cups of tea...

The Parachute Regiment being the aggressive Regiment they are, wouldn't think very much of anybody who got shot, killed or injured. It was their own stupid faults, as they would put it for being there. If they got into the line of a bullet, or if somebody was trying to make a hero of himself, that was just, you know, too bad. When you were shot, you were shot and you shouldn't have been there. That's the way they put things down, you know. Just after internment there was a fair good battle raging in Ballymurphy and it went on for three days. This was the time when Father Mullen was shot going to the assistance of a young boy who'd been shot dead. Consequently Father Mullen died, but when they came back in, I was talking to a medical corporal of the Paras and he talked about this person, a man who had been shot and had been laying in the middle of the road and he had... in his own words he wouldn't give him morphine, a Fenian pig doesn't deserve morphine, and he said he took a kidney out of the dying man, showed it to him and said: "Here you are Fenian bastard, here's your kidney", and threw it away. He was a nurse. Stories like this were very very frequent. They had a good laugh over drinks on them, you know.

I wasn't one-sided till Magilligan. I am one sided now. In the beginning I believed that sometimes the Catholics were as bad as the Protestants. But then again, as things got worse and worse, I believe now that the Catholics, the Catholic workers are definitely oppressed.

The Army have made good by sticking to the one side. Lieutenant Colonel Gray is now a Colonel because of his affectionate meetings with McQuade and the Lord Mayor of Belfast. He used to go and visit him every single morning in the City Hall, for coffee. I cooked for the both of them on numerous occasions. In fact he was a regular visitor to the officers' mess in Palace Barracks. This, I believe, and other officers and men believe, is how he got his promotion. And this is how a lot of officers get promoted in Northern Ireland, sticking with the political scene here, making sure that the Catholic workers don't get too far advanced, keeping the Protestant population happy by running clubs for them. The Tartans for example, who burned the Ardoyne. These were a gang of thugs, they burned the 68 houses in Ardoyne. The parachute regiment ran a club for these thugs, you know. They get food, money for them, they take them on trips...

It got to a stage that I couldn't visit anybody of my family openly. If I wanted to visit my brother, who lives in Ardoyne, I had to make a phone call, tell him when I was coming, ask him if it was alright to come, make sure I wasn't seen going there, by the Army or by the people in the area, because it would have been bad for him and if the Army had seen me it would have been bad for me. My parents-in-law, I didn't visit them very often for the same reasons. My own mother and father moved out of Northern Ireland to go and live in Liverpool because of the situation. Family relations were at the very very minimum.

There was an operation in Derry covered by 39 Brigade. Four battalions in the Brigade, one Paras included, went into Derry at half past four on a Saturday morning and went around burning the cars, letting off one-pound charges, trying to provoke the people into trouble. They brought everything with them, they stayed for 24 hours, even at night, going out screaming and shouting and burning cars and throwing petrol bombs... It didn't succeed. It was in August 71. The Army ran amok to provoke trouble. But the people stayed in their houses.

The Saturday of the Magilligan march three companies of the battalion went out. The evidence was coming back with scraped knuckles, blood streaming from the knuckles when they came back in and had had a really good day of kicking people, punching people, batoning people, for no particular reason at all, you know. Had they wanted to stop the march, they could have stopped it quite peacefully. There was no reason to stop the march, because it wasn't on public ground, it wasn't breaking any of their laws. I think they just went there to have a good punch up. Television showed three paratroopers round one man, kicking him.

It had always been in the back of my mind to leave the Army, because of the situation in Northern Ireland, for about a year. It came to light on a Thursday, when I listened to a conversation in the officer's Mess about what was going to happen in Derry. Personally, even after the conversation I'd overheard, I didn't even believe it myself, I even tried to blot it out of my own mind. There was an O-Group that morning. An O-Group is a Brigade confab, where all the officers of all the battalions in the Brigade come in and have a big pow-wow, you know. Derry was to be an example. They had never been into Derry, they had never been into the Creggan and they were going to go into the Creggan on that particular Sunday. The IRA men, they wanted a confrontation with, and the only way they seemed to be able to get a confrontation was by... to shoot. And shooting they were going to do in Derry on that Sunday which turned out to be the bloodiest Sunday in Ireland's history. The conversation went round to the fact that they were going to shoot innocent people down to get a confrontation with the IRA.

I think the IRA had at that time stated that they would not be in Derry on Sunday, that the march in Derry would be peaceful. I think the Army knew this, that the march would be peaceful, but again, as I say the Army wanted a confrontation in Derry, they wanted to get into Derry, they wanted to hold Derry, as they hold the Falls Road, the New Lodge Road and every other nationalist road and residence in the North of Ireland. Derry was to be broken down. There was to be no more new walls in Derry, as the Creggan had put up walls and barricades. This was the operation in essence: to go in and shoot, to bring the IRA out into the open, to shoot it out with them and to break down the barricades into the Creggan and to occupy the Creggan. I said I didn't believe it. I still don't believe it that it was their real intention to do it... how human beings can think that way, to go in and kill innocent people, it's sort of way beyond me, you know. Although it happened, I believe it happened... but... in the back of my mind I can't really believe it ... that intelligent men could conjure up such a dastardly, vicious, outrageous act... men who are responsible for 700 other men can go out and say: "All right boys we are going out to kill, we'll get these IRA men out and we'll get a really good shoot out". And this was in fact what they were going to do...

I left that Thursday night. That Thursday night I would have been leaving anyway, but after the conversation I'd heard I thought maybe it was time something was done to the paratroopers. They had always had it one sided, their affair had always been to go out and harm and destroy and brutalise the people of Northern Ireland, who till now, although I had been born in Ireland, I hadn't really associated myself with. But now they were my people - my family, my friends - my brothers and sisters who were being brutalised by the Army. It was time that they got some of their own medicine. So, with the help of an organisation which I had got in contact with, I decided that I would give the paras a taste of what they had given to the people of Northern Ireland. Consequently I planted three bombs, each of 25 pounds of gelignite, in the officers' mess and the motor pool. The reason why I had picked the motor pool is because if most of the damage had been done there it would have been unlikely that they would have been able to go to Derry, because of the loss of vehicles. As it happened they were able to get more vehicles in, for the Derry shooting.

But extensive damage was done to the motor pool, extensive damage was done to the garage and extensive damage with severe casualties was done to the officers' mess. At the time the paras, the Parachute Regiment, said they had defused one of the bombs, that very little damage was done and no casualties had been inflicted. But my own wife who had been in the barracks that night and who knew what was going on, not about the bombing, but knew that I was leaving, told me afterwards that ambulances had been coming in for at least an hour afterwards. There had been screaming. It was the loudest bang she had ever heard. And I believe that all three bombs went off and that the Army defused none of them. In fact after the Aldershot bombing, on the 24 Hours programme on BBC, the Army admitted that there had been severe casualties in Palace Barracks, that severe damage had been done to the officers' mess and elswhere. So, in other words, because of the Aldershot explosion, the army had decided that to conceal Palace Barracks would be a bad thing in the light of the sympathy it was getting from Mr. Lynch, the Irish Prime Minister. If they told the world about

Palace Barracks, they would even get more sympathy from Mr. Lynch and Mr. Lynch would have his way open to jail other men, and more men, who are in the South for rest periods from the fighting in the North.

When Derry happened I was moving about in the South. As I say, I didn't believe in what was going to happen in Derry on Sunday, I don't know, maybe why, perhaps I thought it was only boasting, or I didn't think that intelligent men could conjure up such a thing. I didn't know who I could tell, who would be of any good, I hadn't contacted many persons. I said I believed there was going to be severe trouble in Derry, although I didn't say about the killings because I didn't really believe they would do it.

When they had done it, my own personal feelings - I thought that I wanted to get back in, into the North, not caring about any risk or anything, take whatever guns that I had and shoot just all around me, at British soldiers. And I still feel this and I will do everything in my power, with all the knowledge and information I have in fighting, to go back to the North and do my very best to get British troops out of Northern Ireland, once and for all.

I think that after the shooting, in the evening, the paras were very jovial. My wife received a letter, which had been sent out from the commanding officer, about the great job they'd done in Derry, the great victory which would go down in the record book, for the killing of thirteen innocent men. The letter went out to the wives telling them about the great job the Paras had done in Derry and how they rose triumphantly out of this propaganda that they said they were getting. I would have thought that they were very... in fact I know that there would have been a dance in the barracks that night and that they'd be all happy and enjoying themselves and ... have very very little thought for the people of Derry.

Somebody is going to be made a scapegoat for Derry. I believe it will be Colonel Gray, the commander of the Regiment, and I believe that all directions which were given in Derry are going to be thrown on his shoulders. And he is going to take the can for what happened in Derry. He'll be told, very sorry, old chap, you're going to take the can for Derry, but if you look into the records of the Army in two years time, you'll find Colonel Wilford, who is now Colonel Wilford, will be then Brigadier Wilford. Somebody will be the scapegoat, but the Regiment will be made triumphant, for what happened in Derry. I think all political moves will be carried out to make the Parachute Regiment look good. One man will come out and he will be blamed in a very very minute way for what happened in Derry. They'll say he was under great stress, that Colonel Wilford was under great stress, that, when he gave the order to fire, that he was probably up for 48 hours and under mental strain and of course under heavy provocation. It will be a whitewash.

In the Army I wasted nine years. I made up for the waste of nine years in one day, in Palace barracks, by blowing it up. I only wish I could have done more damage. As far as the Army life is concerned, for myself or anybody else who... thinks like me... and has maybe got a little bit of human feeling in his body, to go into the British Army is to go into a slaughterhouse. And it's a waste of time, utterly.

I must give credit to the Army for one thing: that I was well trained in both parachuting, killing, which I'll make good use of against the British Army, and cooking. And I am a good chef and I'll always be able to put my hands back to cooking. My future, I believe, is centred in the South of Ireland because, as I can't move anywhere else except as an elusive person, so I must do a home again and start from scratch with a job and with what little I have left, to make something for my family and something for the people that have suffered in Northern Ireland, and Southern Ireland.

I believe the Army is halfhearted. It's just another job for them, a job a whole lot of them enjoy, but there is no... they have not got the go the IRA has. The IRA has got soul, heart, everything that they own is into their fight for freedom.

And they will win. Ultimately they will win. In the end they will be triumphant, because they have everything: mental power, bodily power, moral power. And they will win. And they will come out triumphant in the very end. The Army have no chance at all. The Army will lose out and the IRA will win. And God help the Army when the IRA really does start the fight, because they haven't really started, they're only tickling. But very very soon I can see the IRA coming out and there will be street conflicts and the IRA will walk away and there will be Bloody Sundays for the Army, because the Army deserve Bloody Sundays, because they are the makers of Bloody Sundays and it's time they felt some of their own medicine.

The IRA envisage a socialist and democratic Republic. I think this is possible, but in Ireland there is lots of nationalistically minded people and possibly in a few years time there will be another conflict within Ireland and this time it will be against Irishmen, for the way of life that they want. Nationalism is a great thing now, but I think socialism is also a great thing, if it can be worked out properly, socialism where you've people working together for the one common good.

They say that Southern Ireland is a socialist country. I say it's not. I say Mr. Lynch is a dictator, the same as Mr. Brian Faulkner, the premier of the North. I am not a politician, I am not a prophet, I can't really say what will happen. I can only say what I'd like to happen. A socialist and democratic republic is one I will fight for.

Dublin, 10th March 1972.

Story of a Sunday afternoon

Bishop's Field, Creggan Estate, Derry,
Sunday, 30th January, 1972. 2:30 p.m.

THE MARCH

Mass is over, Sunday dinner is over, the papers, filled with stories about us, can be read later. Now it's our turn to make the news. New news. New for Derry. We want to have a great day. A day of joy and happiness. And peace. Tomorrow it will be fighting again, surely. Like every day in three years, to keep them at bay, to stay free, to remain ourselves: Sinn Féin. And the gentlemen in duffle coats, with golden parker pens and nosy accents, who every so often peep at us from the gates in the walls, peep at those strange creatures in that strange zoo which calls itself Free Derry, might write again of the 14 year old gunman shot when Bligh's Lane Army post came under attack, or of the nail bomb throwing terrorist who was seen falling at the back of William Street.

Today we march. And march we can, 'cause our streets are free. The gentlemen in duffle coats aren't around. Perhaps they are afraid, or ashamed. Or the Army has kept them behind their barriers, down-

Today we march. And march we can, 'cause our streets are free.

town: one never knows what those hooligans may be up to. Or they are just stuck behind their short drinks in the City "Watch the Bomber Hotel": yet another march, so what.

But what does it matter. The news we make today is for ourselves. And for somebody else, who doesn't need the reports of the duffle coat gentlemen to know what is going on. Somebody up there, in Belfast, or over there, in London who doesn't let a day pass without a little thought for us, for that nasty Derry, for that unbreakable Derry that MUST be broken, just MUST, for you feel it like a cold hole in your well-tailored suit. We want to make that hole larger and larger. That is why we march, straight through it.

How many are we? A few thousand? A few tens of thousands. The field is spilling over. Quite enough to tear that hole a bit wider. And the sun marches with us. Straight from the blue sky. It helps. Helps finding the way through the hole of that well-tailored suit. It shines into the hole and shows up the putrid flesh behind it, crawling with wee little worms in their funny khaki uniforms and hats and poms and leather bridles, looking like circus-ponies dressed up for the big show. Twenty thousand of us can clean up quite a lot of that rotten flesh, tear it away, so that its stench doesn't bother us anymore, up here, in Free Derry.

We are well suited for the job. All fresh and neat in the Sunday suit or dress, bought with the last, faraway pay cheque, when some fat bum over there, in the mill, demanded that we dance with joy for his Friday peanuts, after a week's bloodsucking. And we are all smiles and hallos. There is old Lizzie from Ardoyne, over there the bunch of lads from Armagh, didn't we see them at the Long Kesh march? Twenty thousand of us. Who can stop us, how can they beat us, can we be hurt any longer? Stuff the Army, we are ten times as many. And in nicer spirits. They tell us up there, from the lorry, that we must be peaceful, that everything must be peaceful. No need. We know. Today is a big party. We from Derry and our friends from anywhere, who came out from their miseries, their rubber bullets, their gas, their squalid matchboxes, their Long Kesh buses and dole queues, their baton bashings and raids and spitting, and insults, their tortures and wounds and deaths, to this sunny Sunday of marching and singing and laughing and hoping and believing and knowing, must have a great time. For once, a bloody great time. Peaceful, all right. A festival for ourselves. Sinn Féin. Even the boys of the Movement, who keep us free 24 hours round the clock by patrolling and watching and waking and telling and guarding and shooting and dying young, are in the party, weapons stored away, gazes alert but eyes laughing.

So we move off down the hill, in the sun, hand in hand. A long serpent, Jesus so long, never seen anything like it. Those creeps on the walls must have butterflies around their bellies. What if we decided to rip the while well-tailored suit apart. But that's for later. For tomorrow. With guns. More and more guns. How many of these 20,000 would love to carry one now. But now we are holding hands, and that's even better. We shall not be moved and, better still, we shall overcome. And soon, soon, we shall just march on and on, until we all reach Dublin, in the green, in the green, ourselves and all the men behind the wire.

The tail is in Creggan and the top down, below the cemetery of young Lafferty and Cusack, in the Bogside. Who do we want to free — every last internee. Barricade after barricade. Hands linked. Easy job for the stewards. Grannies and babies at little front doors, waving and smiling, being waved and smiled at. All the others in the march, boys, men, girls. All our lot. Something you can be proud and confident about. For three years they have threatened, shot, besieged us. Now Ireland is here and besieges them.

Past all those wee houses, clutched together in huddling rows, wee walls that we keep painting with fresh colours, pink, grey, brown, yellow. Walls around wee rooms with lots of Long Kesh hankies, pictures of dead and interned, tricolours and Connolly flags and little else. They don't look so poor now, the wee houses with their neatly painted walls, full of laughing faces. Down William Street, singing and chanting, stewards buzzing around. Pigs well away, behind corners, lurking. Hey there, limeys. Good day for

...that huge monster ... with the thin barrel...
...the watercannon keeps spraying.

There they go again drenching the place with gas.

killing, you said this morning. Good day for marchin' and singin' and showing you how many we are, all feeling the same. Drop dead, limeys. Quiet boys, peaceful, no trouble, leave them alone today. Oh well, see you, limeys, tomorrow.

WILLIAM STREET

Now the stewards seal off the road. Everybody turn right, behind the lorry and the banner and Ivan Cooper, MP. Further down the road are the rubber bullets. And he, Ivan, has had his share of rubber bullets. One straight on the head the other day, at Magilligan. Was worth it, though. The barrier had been swept away, on the beach, and the internees were going mad in the camp: climbing on the roofs of the cages, letting the gale have a go at the tricolour. We know our rubber bullets. Catch them in the air, paint them white, orange and green and put them on the mantelpiece. We know our gas, kick or throw it back at the bastards, pour sand on it, got used to that filthy breath, have it everyday, will grow immune to it, like flies to DDT. May even get addicted — gives us a kick.

But many, most, go on, behind the lorry and Cooper, up to Free Derry Corner where the meeting will be. Can we leave those limeys alone? What are they there for, anyway? What's that barrier for? We don't have to have barriers in our place. Where there is a barrier, there has to be a challenge. They have learned this. They know that if they left us alone, there would be nothing to challenge, to attack. They want us to challenge. Why should those Fenians have a good day, some clean air?

Forget the clean air. We'll show them. We don't take barriers, no Irishman takes barriers. We are free. What do you mean with that barrier at the bottom of William Street? The slums and the fields for us, and the nice city, the glamorous cinemas, the fat shops, the touristy buildings for you? You must be joking. What are we, some kind of suburban lepers to be kept off limits? Let's at least tell them what we think of their barriers, what we are going to do to their barriers tomorrow.

They have gone to town all right. Barbed wire, riot gear, batons, a wall of Saracens and then that huge monster behind, with the thin barrel. Must be some watercannon. How many of us? Hundred, hundred and fifty perhaps, and no little toys to get going with. It's just not on. But, anyway, let's give them a few nice words. Hey, limeys, what's that barrier for? Having the shit scared out of you, what? Why don't you just go home, pack up and fuck off...

What do you make that ass-face for? You an officer, hey? Well go, and office somewhere else. We want to get into our town, like, want some chips, do you mind? "This is an illegal march. You will not be allowed through this barrier." Ho, ho, ho. Must have forgotten who we are. Illegal to you and all the creepy bastards like you. Not illegal to us. There are 20,000 of us. Who do you think made this city? Go home to Manchester and grow your shrubs. We want to get through here.

Nothing doing. Some surprise. But let's keep pricking them a wee bit more. It's rubber bullets already? Must be in a nasty mood. Rubber bullets all over the place. Gas too. Let's get out of here. Up William Street. More gas. It's filthier than usual, must have some new cook out of hell. And the monster is coming out too. Has that limey gone mad or something? We are all running away anyway. Probably wants a festival himself. That dirty water, mauve or something, gets everywhere. Icy and filthy. Mucks up the good suit. Everybody running away, back to the Bogside. And the watercannon keeps spraying. People are stumbling, falling over.

A girl too, another one. A proper stampede. Must be like this when they go berserk at one of those football matches in South America and thousands get trampled to death. Awful feeling, lying on the ground, in a puddle of mauve dirt, in a cloud of CS, banged at with rubber bullets and trampled over by a crowd that behaves like some buffalo herd off from the fire.

The street is cleared. Better go back to Free Derry Corner. But wait, something going on down the road, in the yard

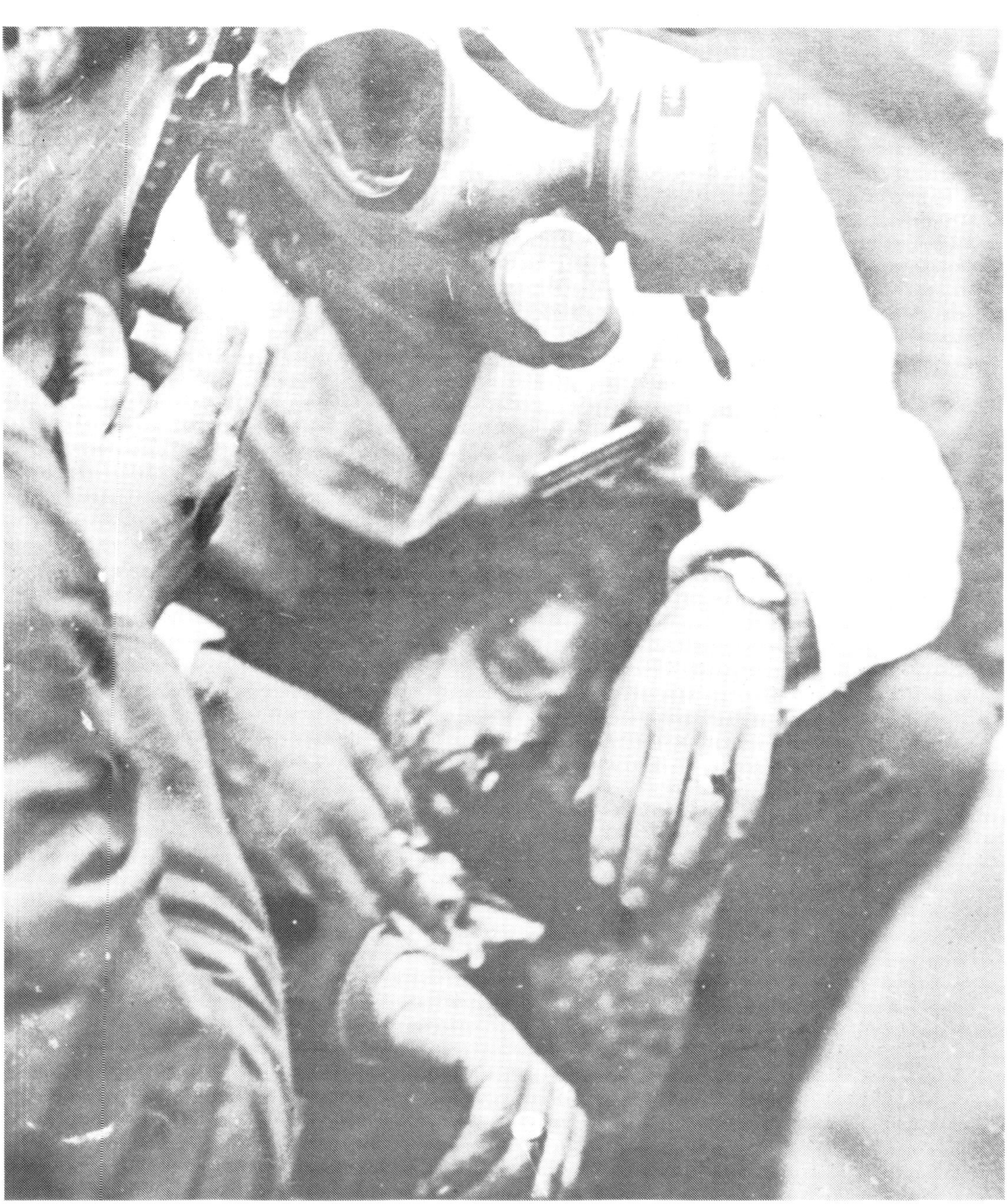

unreal gasmask close to the all too human white face... stop the blood...

towards Sackville Street. A dozen lads having another go at the bastards. Clever move, though, advancing towards the pigs behind corrugated metal shields and, from about thirty yards, throwing the rock. But there are too few of us. Let's wait for a better opportunity. There they go again, drenching the place with gas. It's a volley of about a dozen this time, plus a rosary of rubber bullets. But is it rubber bullets? Had an odd sound this time. Like high velocity guns. Out, out. Can't breathe. Everybody's running, coughing, screeching. Filthy stuff; burns your lungs right off. Can't see a thing. Eyes like in a bush of nettles. Let's hope the limeys are not having a go just now. Wouldn't know where to dive. Would probably end up straight under a pig. Got to get over to the High Flats. Everybody is over there anyway. Might as well have that "peaceful meeting".

THE MASS MURDER

It is 4 o'clock. One more hour's light for pictures, if these damned eyes open up again and the cough relents. Never had so much gas in about a hundred outbursts of state-poison. Tripping and falling about, I almost end up under the gush of vomit of some woman. Several people are vomiting. The others are all coughing their lungs out. We are in that waste bit of land between a burnt out house facing William Street, and the courtyard of Rossville Flats. Facing the flats, there is Rossville Street at the right and the houses that open up on Chamberlain Street on the left. We are huddled around the entrance to Eden Street, some 20 yards of road up into Chamberlain Street. Who has somehow recovered, moves on to Free Derry Corner.

There is suddenly a commotion near the corner of Rossville Street and William Street. The horizon is a wall of white gas, lingering in the still air, and beneath, like escapees from some underworld, a group of men, four or five, tries to make its way in our direction, through a still coughing and spluttering crowd. The concern with one's own condition suddenly, instinctively, gives way to something more serious: there must be somebody REALLY ill, for the group of men appear to be carrying a body. As we approach, a sudden scream of a woman:
"It's a real bullet!"
"No, no, it's only rubber."
"I think it's a gas canister."
"No rubber bullet causes that kind of gash."
More voices, shouts, three or four layers of people around the body. Also some first aid people with gas masks. Following them, we get through to the injured. A boy. Long blond hair. He has been laid down, but a nurse is holding up his head: a mask of blood. Blood pouring from under the nose and from the mouth, all over the face, into the neck, on the shirt, in the long curly hair. Blond and red. The face white, whiter. Eyes half closed, dazed. A first aid man, unreal gasmask close to the all too human white face, tries to stop the blood with some white cloth: an island of white in the dark huddle of Sunday suits. But within seconds the white is all red again. Must take a picture. A picture of a wounded man has always eluded me.

The group and us, with the boy again lifted in a makeshift stretcher of arms, moves on to the little passage that is Eden Street. Calls for an ambulance. Helpless expressions. Everybody looks around. No telephone till Chamberlain Street.

4:05 pm. There are no more than about a hundred people left in Rossville Square. Perhaps twenty on our side, near the entrance to Eden Street. For the second time the wall of white poison growing up from William Street is suddenly broken. Grey, dark, bulky forms rapidly growing into more precise contours and shapes, advancing at unbelievable speed, shooting out in all directions, one coming straight at us, another one speeding down Rossville Street towards the Flats and the tiny barricade at the end of the Flats.

One moments hesitation and incredible silence. Then scattering, running, shouting, falling, getting up, tripping again, pushing, pushing harder into barriers of flesh, shouting on, trying to reach the safety of the Flats, or behind the Flats, or of Eden Street. But no panic yet, no despair, no astonishment: the usual dispersion under a coming

onslaught of gas, or rubber bullets, or batons. Enough gas, enough dyed water, enough rubber bullets for today. It hasn't been that bad for some time. Nobody is prepared. No hankies, no vinegar, nor any more banners to turn into sticks.

On our side, cut off as we are from the main escape route towards the Free Corner, there is a mad rush towards Eden Street, which squeezes us in and turns the street into a thick human sausage. I don't want to be trampled on again, like under the waterspray in William Street, and stay behind, among the last, with Susan, who turns her tape on, for more rubber bullet bangs, for more hissing of gas. And I want to see the scene through the reflex, in order to get anything worthy on film.

The Saracens career into the square and stop, scattered at some twenty yards one from the other. Perhaps three or four of them. Loud bangs of the backdoors opened fast against the metal body, crouching figures leaping out of the inner darkness with long, thin weapons in their hands, and running left and right, mostly forward, behind the fleeing crowd. It shoots through my mind: this will look like an American war film, Yokohama or something. Same characters: men under extreme determination, operating like machines, like little military robots in a perfect war game. Helmets tied with double straps to the chin, camouflage, black gas masks, things round their belts, weapons, leaping crouching, running.

Why? We weren't throwing anything. None of the boys had been throwing stones or bottles any more. Reprisal? For what? The stoning and yelling of before was a mini copy of what happens in William Street regularly, normally, every day. And this time there hadn't even been a single nailbomb, a single petrol bomb. Our tape recording was singularly poor: only gas and rubber, not one decent explosion.

Why? An ever growing why. And we were all drifting away from the trouble area, we were all sick and eager to get out. There was only gas left.

Why? What were they after? A quick snatch operation, to make a few boys pay for the immeasurable humiliation of three miles of broken ban?

But then, again, why? Why these soldiers different from all the others, different from those that one coped with daily at the 3 o'clock riots in William Street, different from the ones of earlier, behind the barrier, different from any soldier, at any time? Why no shields, or batons; why no big short rubber bullet guns, or screens on the helmets?

Paratroopers. The helmet, round and bulky like a casserole, proved it. But why paratroopers in a Rossville Square filled with tired, coughing, poisoned, soaked, fleeing people? What the hell do they want? The camera would see. Peering through the reflex, I follow one of the leaping figures from the Saracen. He jumps out, runs a few yards to the right, towards Rossville Street, turns, runs up towards the courtyard of the Flats, stops, lifts the carbine to his shoulder, looks for a split second over to another paratrooper, ten yards to the left, in identical position, fires, his head swinging slightly back, fires again, another shock of the head, fires again. Then starts running again.

Another one, chasing a boy with a handkerchief on his face; the boy falls; the paratrooper steps over him, on him; stops; points the rifle from 10 inches into the contorted mass from which an arm raises, to shield, to plead; fires - the mass jerks, lays still. Another one: grabbing a small, oldish, fleeing fellow, lifting the baton, smashing it down - smash, smash, smash... on head, shoulders, back, head.

I clicked once, twice. Another one - black gasmask, helmet, camouflage - turns round, points the gun at me, from the hip, from ten yards.

Somebody pulls me from behind, forcefully, the second click goes off while I am falling backwards, I stagger, follow the pull, the pull lets go, I walk backwards, then run backwards, then turn, see Susan at the top of Eden Street with her hands stretched out, shouting something to me, still holding the microphone. I run. Everybody around me runs. Not a word. Only shuffle and trampling then.

Only life in mind. Screams mounting into a tornado a little further away. Come on, lad! Somebody passing and pushing at my right shoulder, to pass, to help.

The Why that had grown as big as the whole square suddenly shrinks to the dimension of a carbine. And the answer comes like a frantic hiccup: as if a Saracen is having the hiccups after vomiting. Bang, bang, bang, bang, bang, bang-bang, bang.

And every bang followed by a little ranting, a hoarse hiss: kchhhh, kchhhh...

Why? The answer is fired at you by some thirty or forty minute men, wrapped up in comic inspired clothes of virility and power, altogether unbelievably grotesque and ridiculous, like all soldiers anywhere, and more so. Little stuffed men, incapable of speaking, of looking into your face and seeing your eyes, incapable of hearing and listening, incapable of understanding and knowing. Little robots programmed on the use of a gun against a target. Little toys out of some magic box concocted by the mad scientist to help him become the master of all men and the owner of all Earth, told to march out, like human beings, then to jump, like human beings, to run a bit, like human beings, to go down on one knee, like human beings, to lift their little deadly stick and make bang-kchhhh, bang-kchhhh, against real human beings.
IT'S LIVE!...

The scream hit louder than all the explosions. It hit and stunned. It's live. And suddenly we were faced with death. It wasn't a question of sores, bruises, lung congestion, freezing water any more. It was death or life. The absolute alternative. For everybody. Those with camera and press card included. As never before, more than political and human affinity and solidarity had ever achieved, we, observers, reporters, uninvolved parties, were part of the one side, the people's side. And we accepted the identification, automatically, naturally. The mechanism of death was after us too, ready to catch up, grind, obliterate. The alternative of running in the opposite direction, away from the people who had to be killed. Behind the barriers of safety and officialdom, of "impartiality", didn't even cross our minds. And it certainly wasn't because this side of the fence better professional opportunities were offered, the prospect of some unique scoop, recognition, popularity, money. The message that those live bullets carried directly to you, did away with that. It was just that we felt, without thinking, without rationalising, that we belonged to the running and screaming and falling and dying and hating and despairing: the people, and not the ludicrous little death-spitters that invisible strings made hop around and chase and shoot and kill. As simple as that. And a deep perception ran underneath all, realised only much later at the level of conscience, that it had always been like this and would always be. Now, more than ever before.

"The bastards are shooting live..." It had to be seen, again, better. To know, to understand, to tell, to fight better tomorrow. For a moment I lost sight of Susan. I just saw her, mike waving, expression strained by the most utter astonishment I had ever seen in a familiar face, moving with the tide of the crowd along Eden Street, towards the place of mass executions, as we later saw. Then I ran back, to the corner of Eden Street and the square. One or two minutes had passed. The firing was getting hectic, like one, long burst.

I saw the back of the paratroopers. Almost all were facing the courtyard besieged on three sides by the towering flats: the ideal place for a massacre. Some were kneeling and aiming, others were standing and aiming, others yet were darting towards the street in an effort to cut off the escape route of those few who had been overtaken by the roaring monsters as they sped in. The tiny monsters — and I keep remembering the paratroopers as tiny, artificial, mechanical, and the people as normal sized, or even larger than life. People in fact was almost all I saw, perhaps I wanted to see. The killers had diminished to dimensions of crawling lizards — had black gasmasks on their blackened, irresponsible faces. The humans had big, white faces, tense with effort and purpose: the purpose of running, of getting to safety. There wasn't room yet for horror. Small crouching, bouncing, death-spluttering insect-faced science fiction monsters, after men, human beings.

I saw a young man running, then slowing down and looking over, where an old grey-haired man was limping frantically away, sliding into slimy puddles of poison-drenched rainwater, nearly falling backwards, raising his arms, waving for leniency and compassion. The youth leaped over, put his arm under the old man's, pulled him on. Five yards to his right, a little further on, a boy with short, dark hair, lifted his hand to his face as he raced past one of the killers. Should he be shot, he didn't want to see. The mercenary let him go past, glanced down at his weapon, settled something on it with his hand, moved a few steps forward, calmly, lifted the carbine to his shoulder, pointed with the black barrel at the back of the fleeing boy, calmly. Shot. Calmly...

A helmet shone under the sun and caught my eye. The area in front of me was getting deserted. Everything had moved on towards the Flats. The glimmer on the helmet bounced up and down as its owner ran after a tiny, unreal group. A man in his older years, but tall and incredibly erect, with a cap on his white head, walking stealthily in his own direction, towards Rossville Street, away from the mainstream of chased and pursuers. Close to him, holding him up in a gesture that he didn't seem to need, a girl nurse, in her white coat the most evident object in all the blurred, moving scene. They were the only ones who weren't running, not even hurrying. Just walking, slowly, step-by-step, without turning, looking. Firm and erect. Courage and dignity.

The events had by-passed my position. I turned and ran up Chamberlain Street. Just in time... from the William Street end more Saracens were moving in, with soldiers flanking and following on foot, guns at the ready. Germans mopping up some Warsaw ghetto, I reflected. And as I hurried up the street, the glimpse of childhood fantasy shot through my mind: when, walking along narrow alleys, I imagined some huge ice-breaking vessel moving up the road, with steel pushers wiping away whatever they met on the way, and I tried to figure some way of getting away, flying up perhaps, and ended up with images of smashed flesh, of bones crunched against the walls flanking the street, and dreaded the thought that this icebreaker should ever come true. There it was, slowly and horribly moving up the street, determined to crush anything. Come true.

Susan was waiting at the top of the street, among the last of the fleeing. She was pressing against the wall and shouted: "Can't you see, they are here too, they are coming up, can't you see, Fulvio watch out, Fulvio..." I got to her. "Keep the tape recorder going." Keep everything going. We MUST keep going. We are the ones that can tell, that get listened to. We must tell. Tell about them, tell what is being done to them, human beings, our human beings, our friends, our smiles, our handshakes, our time, our shelter, our confidence and trust. We ARE them. Keep going.

I find a way to the corner which opens up on the courtyard. There is no movement, no running now. Everything transfixed, still. Only bang-kchhhh, ... bang-kchhhh. One starts reacting, registering at level of conscience. One is still alive. One feels the wave inside coming, mounting, spilling over. "You bastards... stop it, stop it..." In front of them, looking at them, madly. Perhaps some unconscious feeling still that your camera, your ridiculous press card makes you invulnerable. The science fiction toy in front points his black insect trunk at me, aims, fires. Later they tell me, three times. Forceful arms grab me again, pull me back: "You out of your mind or something?", "He's cracked up, they almost got him". People still manage to think of other people. Of helping them to be alive, and happy, and walking, eating, talking, thinking, suffering, hating, loving, giving, taking.

The insects are only one big, monolithic thought, wrapped in khaki and lawfulness: kill, hit, hurt, eliminate. Somebody carries a woman past me. A trail of blood behind. Lumps of flesh, red, grainy, like strawberry jelly, dangling from her thigh(1).

A man like an hallucination, clear and high in the dazzling confusion of impres-

(1) Margaret Deery, 37 years, 15 children).

sions, blonde, moustached, thin, towards the middle of the square, the cesspool of death. Raises his arms: "Shoot *me*, you bastards... Shoot me, not women, not a mother of 15 children." Demanding logic, even understanding and compassion, humanity, from mechanical insects with black trunks that were told to sting. Sting anybody till they fall and die. Up to thirty. "Thirty is the limit", somebody heard the chief insect yelling. Thirty. Thirteen dead, sixteen wounded, one woman killed by a heart attack at the perception of the horror. Thirty. Perfect mechanised insects. The man who shouted crumbles to a heap and slowly stretches out. Like the gradual deflating of a balloon. A bullet hit him in the knee. Serves you as a lesson. Who are we to tell the difference between a mother of fifteen and anyone else?

Susan and I follow the man in the house at the left-hand side corner of Chamberlain Street. Commotion inside, but subdued. Two wounded have to be attended. Also, the mother is here. On a couch in the living room. Moans, weeps, can't understand. Why so much pain, so much, the leg coming off, so much pain? For what?

Somebody wraps a towel round the torn thigh, presses the big lump back into place. But it won't fit, spills all over. So much pain. For what? British people, for what?

The moustached man lies in the courtyard, head on somebody's lap, long and stretched out, his trousers lowered on one side. No panic. Concern. Efforts for some organisation. Help, save, alleviate: everybody around has this thought. And he, he doesn't want to be attended. Knows that there are others in worse condition. Waves off smiles and hands. Doesn't want to be hurt. Doesn't want to show pain. Smiles more than all the others. His hurt leg trembling wild. Then his own body trembling and shaking. To his annoyance. Every effort in controlling the shaking. Not the pain. The pain isn't even there, friends.

Bang-kchhhh, bang-kchhhh. Going on and on. Nobody has pushed the stopping button on the mechanical insects yet, like on some alarm clock. Programmed on shooting, to the end of the magazines. Up to thirty. The sacred, official number. Consecrated in London, in the dungeons of the mad scientist.

We must get out again. The commotion has become a whisper. Nothing must add in the slightest to the ill-being of the hurt. Yet, how many desperate worries. How many friends and brothers and sisters and fathers and dear ones out there, in the hell, perhaps never to come back or to be the same again?

Whisper, silence, as the dark shadow of the monster appears behind the front door window. A Saracen outside the house. They have made their way up the road. God save us. A pole is firmly planted against the door handle. The shadow doesn't move. Everybody stares at it through the dimming glass. Like a television screen gone stuck and who knows what happens next.

But we must get out, we must see, record. "They are going to come in and kill us all. Don't go. And they are going to kill you. Do you think they want the press to see this and tell the world? Don't go." When I attempt to climb over the backyard wall, somebody opens the door. A woman decides to get an ambulance, come what may. The Saracen is there. Heavy and still, like a big beast after its meal. A soldier at the side of the door. Not a paratrooper. "Press. We want to go on." The man in khaki doesn't seem to grasp. His eyes are fixed, wide open, his mouth too. Does he wobble or is it imagination? "Yeah, Yeah..." he mumbles, not knowing it. His well trained head hasn't been trained well enough. The horror got him. Horror inflicted on others, of all things, on hooligans, terrorists, snipers. Needs some revisioning. Isn't mechanised enough yet.

A group of about twenty, mainly boys, some girls in fresh Sunday dresses, for the great march, now all stained and creased and forgotten, huddled against the corner of the concrete wall that runs from the backside of Chamberlain Street to the small arcade leading from the courtyard to the back of the flats, where Joseph Place opens up towards Free Derry corner. They didn't make it to the back of the flats, to the corner where 20,000 would have certainly kept you safe against death, warm against horror, to

A first aid boy... near the body... lifting the head gently... a priest... another man

the corner which was life, and as dear as life, to which every little atom in you, fleeing, pulled you, called you, urged you. They had been cornered. The paratroopers had come into the courtyard and had stopped at its front line, so as to be able to sow death impartially, both in the yard and towards the street. So as to close the death trap. Only the arcade was open: amusing for target practice. As soon as one dares the passage to life, bang-kchhhh.

The boys squeeze desperately into the corner. The corner doesn't give away. The bullets fly nearer and nearer. They are huddling like small, young frightened animals under the onslaught of the hurricane. Feet pushing against the concrete path to get into the mount of life and cover. Feet slipping.

Feet and head drawn in, to shrink, disappear. There, at twenty yards, the arcade. Beyond; life. Between here and there an invisible buzzing, clanging wall of death, the passage into nothing. Bullets ricocheting from the concrete wall.

In the middle of the yard a small body(1), with outstretched arms, face to the sky, head to the Flats. Like on the cross. Under the hail vomited by the filthy insects, heroes come to life and to unforgettable memory. A first aid boy, in the uniform of his duty, in the spirit of his love. Kneeling near the body, lifting the head gently: white, thin face framed in black, a young boy's face, as clean as the early sky, as empty of life. Eyes slowly fading away, back into himself. A priest crawling towards the two, and then another man.

I wave a white handkerchief and go to the group. Get down on my knees, want to see, pale face, half open mouth, eyes back into himself, whiter, whiter still, tattered pullover, poor boy's pullover, slipped up, white chest, fragile, vulnerable, white skin, skin of a living boy, skin without blood gradually, chest without air, slack, thin stomach, caving in, poor boy's stomach, delicate, weak. I see between the shoulder of the priest and the first aid man, see like through a pipe because of the two leaning over Kevin, or perhaps because I am looking through the reflex, to see better, to make you all see. Never to forget. To know what to do. To them. The murderous sub-humans. The soulless mechanical tools. And their masters, the mad, frothing, mad scientists.

The priests kneels. He raises his right hand. He drops it. His mouth is strained like in a forced smile. He weeps. He raises his hand again and draws a cross over Kevin, weeping.

I didn't know then. I now remember that it was then and there that I changed the film. Automatically. Subconsciously obeying through the means of experience and conditioned reflexes the one imperative: keep going. At least beat them by one photograph. One more picture than bullets.

The men lift Kevin in their arms. There is a hole in the back of his thigh and one in his shoulder. The same bullet. The sort of ammunition one would use for elephants.

The priest raises a white handkerchief which drops with blood saying: Kevin is dead, Kevin has been killed by you. Now let us through. Wrath bigger than any fear of monster, however nightmarish. Now death is with us. We have it in our arms. Nothing can hurt us any more. Not all those bullets buzzing over our heads, past our ears.

A perfect opportunity for whoever exists in a condition where the values of life and death, of love and destruction, have been turned upside down. A great occasion for the mechanical insects. As the group gets going towards the entrance of Chamberlain Street the firing livens up. Perhaps they don't want to kill us now, just a little scare. We may as well know that a dead boy means nothing to insects. Whether he has a clean face and a vulnerable little chest or not. Whether those people carrying him, limp and so weak, so completely weak, to somewhere beyond strife and even crime and murder, are men, heroes, and you, just tiny black nothings with trunks, capable only of doing bang-kchhhh, or not.

(1) Kevin McElhinney, 16 years

The priest bends down and keeps his bloody handkerchief high, the others proceed at his side. The bullets keep getting directed at us. The priest bends lower, hankie still high, goes into a crouch, handkerchief on the ground to support him. The bullets fly lower. Then suddenly, before being finished like worms crawling on the ground, we all get up together, straight, forward. And are invulnerable. A scream, unbelievably loud: "You see now what the British Army is like?"

I am back at the huddle of fright in the corner, where Susan is waiting, unbelievable in her absence of fear, microphone recording for the world the sounds of murder. It is crazy to remain here, where one boy has already been shot dead(1), his blood is all over the place, and as the feet in the huddle draw away from it and from exposure, it follows, slowly expanding, lingering around heels and hands, meaning you must get away, take a chance, save yourself.

The huddle of scared to death humanity is the only living thing in the area. For some moments nothing seems to move. Then suddenly the SS Panzers get going again. Slowly now they rumble on. Some three, deeper into the courtyard, slowly, horribly, appearing from behind the corner at the back wall of Chamberlain Street, getting bigger and bigger, they can now aim at the huddle in the corner above, which squeezes against the wall, squeezes, squeezes, hopelessly. It will only be a matter of seconds before the beasts can rain death upon the huddle. Other grey monsters move on, along Rossville Street, towards the first barricade of Free Derry, and vanish behind the towering grey mass of the Flats.

Everything is grey. The preposterous thought that it is just as well that I have only black and white film crosses the blurred mind. The huddle at the end of the concrete wall, a pyramid of white and black, fading into grey, black Sunday suits, white shirts, white faces, white of wide eyes, a pyramid literally piling up against the corner, is a trembling mass of grey gelatine, melting away towards the footpath and then frenziedly freezing up again, solidifying into the corner again. The high walls of the blocks of flats, all those grey, blind windows, pour grey onto the ccurtyard, engulfing insects and their Panzers, drenching the air and the soil with grey. Sunless air, skyless air. Livid. Or maybe the eyes see grey, because the blood, feelings, thoughts, are all getting grey. Some days later I shall have a grey dream: grey, huge, dust-grey curtains descending from nowhere into nowhere, and I filter through, into nowhere, wide nowheres, and then grey curtains again, and grey nowheres, endlessly. Death? And eventually, in the middle of nowhere, between four endless grey curtains, on a grey, soft, delicate bed of grey, a white pearl, shining and throwing a halo a few inches around it.

There is no perception of sound, then. But the urge to move. Not to be squashed into a mass of torn flesh in that dreadful corner. Like a bunch of mice. What is there, between us and the other end of the footpath along the concrete wall, the arcade, the passage, the back of the High Flats? A dash, or eternity?

At the edge of the huddle, a trickle, slow, tentative. A few men crawl away, on their fours, like ants, eyes fixed on the passage beyond the Flats. And beyond, death. A row of three, four. Crawling. God, maybe we'll make it. Just 10 yards, 8, 6. Crackles, hissing... bullets again. The last in the row jerks to the side.

His jacket jerks up, falls back, limp. He breaks down, onto his elbows. But holds on, carries on. Like a horse that stumbled over a barrier, and doesn't want to give up. Which would mean, to die. Another crackle. Another jerk. Terror eyes from the corner spilling over him, urging him on, with all the love for life. And he crawls on, wriggles on. Makes it.

I pull Susan to my side, lift that handkerchief again, lift the camera, push on towards the Earth, out of hell. Look back, wave to the huddle, it dissolves little by little, raises into distinct figures, figures moving behind us, cautiously, then with more conviction, faster, along the path, along the wall, like a wall for an execution squad, grey.

(1) Jack Duddy, 17 years

I look back again, towards the corner at the back of Chamberlain Street, where the monsters lurk. I see a man, or is it an insect, with his little deadly pipe pointed at us, looking straight at me. Squeeze Susan to me. Suddenly the thought of her face still, motionless, like little Kevin's, squeezes my stomach in a hard, painful grip. I don't want to see her like that. God, no. Please, if you must, shoot at me. Please, you bastards, please.

All of a sudden, sound again. Loud, powerful, maddening sound. The huddle of before is all on its feet. Susan, in front with me, turns half way and urges them on. Come, come, fast, for Christ's sake, fast. They are not shooting now. And the sound grows, furiously, uncontrollable. Fear into anger. The total risk is taken. And with the total risk, life is there, with all its extreme power. And with life, anger, contempt, rage. Things stronger than death. The paratroopers at the corner stand like salt figures. Paralysed. Uncomprehending, in front of total courage out of total despair.

They can't figure it out. A crowd of defenceless, hopeless, completely vulnerable people, at the prolonged end of the barrel that can give death in the flicker of a mood, yelling, defying, cursing, weeping and not giving a damn. Murderers, bastards, come on, shoot, kill, bastards, BASTARDS.

Just before the passage, five feet away from it, a step. Men crouching in frozen fear, but now hearing the storm of strength, rising, walking away, come what may. One, big, forceful, un-rolling from under the step, getting between me and Susan, taking our hands, weeping, smiling, squeezing our hands, thank-you, thank-you, I'll come with you, thank-you. And as we file through the passage, under the arcade, then under a little bridge from one block to the other, slowly, composed; others at the other end, alongside the block of flats, who had been lying against the wall, where the wall blocked their escape, get up as they see us, move towards us and our immunity, in single line, one by one, slowly, almost unbelievingly.

And here is when insect machinery gone stuck, starts grinding again. The hitting, the killing-conditioning of the programme reasserts itself. Ideal line-up for target practice, one target after the other, in a row, slowly moving on, like in rifle ranges in fun fairs. Like that white bear in the electronic rifle range, that screams and gets up on its hind feet when hit in that glass hole on his belly. "Don't shoot, don't shoot." Cry into empty space, to empty shells of insects, everlasting.

Bang-kchhhh, bang-kchhhh... three, four, five. Of our group almost everybody has gone through the passage. Down there, though, a girl screams and falls, a boy, some steps ahead, throws his arms into the air and plunges. Bang-kchhhh...

Another boy, three feet from the passage and from me clutches his side, looks at me wide-eyed, bewildered, drops onto himself in a pile, stretches slowly out, crawls on. Bang-kchhhh. In a row, faster all the time. Chips from the wall fly around my head. Bullets into the wall make small instant whirls of stone-dust, in a row.

Round the corner, at the back of Rossville Flats. Over there. Free Derry Corner. And a moving grey mass away from it, like lava and cinders pouring from the fire hole, some cinders falling away, little human figures that panic drew from the mass, melting frantically into it again.

Round the corner, at the back of the strong, good, familiar High Flats. Not in waste ground any more, not along lifeless concrete walls. But where shops are, normal, everyday life, words, smiles. So normal and familiar that nothing crazy can happen to you here. Round the corner, where normal, warm life is, always. We made it.

Round the corner. Three people dead. Stretched out in a line, with large gaps in between. Two with their heads towards Free Derry Corner and their feet towards the flats. One the other way round. And all along the front of the flats, under the arcade, people, pressed against the wall, like in that corner of before. It's

still going on, the same thing. And we must keep going. Body and mind work like a machine, anticipated reflection and impression. Thank heavens for that.

TARGET PRACTICE. DEATH FROM THE WALLS.

People still dying. My people, our people. Our friends, our good, generous, warm, brave, innocent, loved friends. All us. Sinn Féin. Five yards from the passage the body of a man in his working clothes. (1)

A terrorist with a gun? A sniper so good that he could fire through thirty feet of flats at the oncoming soldiers, which he couldn't see, and had to be neutralised? A hooligan, master-butcher Ford, who was throwing "ugly things" over ten stories of concrete? No. The man who crawled for life. Whom they hit, hit, hit, 'cause he would keep crawling. And he made it. And died. Courageous, brave, able insects, defending society, serving civilisation. Massacring the just. Murdering the innocent. Assassinating the unseen, from safe positions.

The steel containers of the insects haven't reached the Rossville corner of the Flats yet. One of these was killed from high above, from the walls of the rich and the greedy and their armed servant insects. As he was running to his free city, to life.

It is silence again. Only bang-kchhhh, bang-kchhhh, somewhere, not too near. When I register the necessity to go, to see what has happened to that body, there aren't three bodies yet. Only one, near us. But before I can move, a man (2) emerges from the rows along the flats, tentatively, towards the same object. His head sticks out eagerly to find life, please, life, in the huddle of untidy clothes, in the widening puddle of blood. His hand waves, pleading for truce. Then his head swings to the side, like under a forceful fist blow. Swings back, but slacker, and the movement is picked up by the whole figure. A spin, arms flying wide out, a step for balance, crumbling and gliding out, on the back. Parallel to the first body.

Two bodies. And now another figure makes a move out of the dark mass in the shadow of the arcade. To help. Flat out on his stomach, only head slightly raised, wriggling, crawling, more wriggling, stopping, bang-kchhhh, bang-kchhhh, head down, buried in the concrete of the pavement, wriggling again, alone, unbelievable, against all odds, against all chances of life, which don't matter, because the one, small chance of life in that still body, or is there a slight movement? Matters infinitely more.

These are people who just HAVE to be murdered. Susan keeps recording. A sobbing boy, perhaps 17-18, in her arms. Recording panting, whispering, " how many do they want to kill, for Christ's sake, how many? bastards, the BASTARDS", recording on, yells of hysteria, again mounting shouts of rage, frustration, questions, imploring questions, why, why are they doing this to us...

That useless, ridiculous handkerchief in hand, I walk towards the first dead, or is he still dying? Or is he just wounded? Handkerchief slips out of hand. I bend down to pick it up. I am near the body and remain in a squatting position.

They tell me later that when bending to pick up the handkerchief, three bullets in rapid succession pass just over me, into the wall. They show me the wall, later, with the three holes... two crunched bullets. Must be the three rounds that master-butcher Ford claimed his boys had fired, at 6pm, on BBC-TV.

This man is almost dead. Slight up and down of his chest, a little froth around his mouth, a yellow-green bubble which grows, slowly, slowly, and then bursts, spittle dangling from the lower lip, lingering, dropping from the chin. Another bubble trying to form between the half-parted lips. Not making it. Dead.

The wriggling figure moves on, is almost there.

Wriggles over to the dead body. Applies his mouth to the dead mouth. Blows his

(1) Patrick Doherty,
(2) Bernard Mc Guigan, 41 years.

breath in. Blows and blows into the dead body. Presses his hands on a cold chest, releases, presses again. The dead chest. The dead mouth. The dead body. The dead human being. The man without thirty, forty years of sun and rain, love and song, sleep, dream and movement. With death only.

His eyes are gone into his forehead. It is all the white there is. The face is yellow, getting more yellow all the time. Horribly yellow. Insects make you so ugly. Another crime.

When I get up, after a few steps towards Rossville Street, another body. Belly down, lifts his head, stares into my face.

"How are you?", "I'm alright, can't move. The bastards keep shooting. Go On." "Watch it." "You watch it, too."

More, lying like him. Who is dead, who feigns death not to be dead?

Then the man who wanted to help and pleaded with his hand. A big mass, heavy, dark, worn suit. Big face. Face without its left side. Without an eye. The eye got projected against the wall by elephant ammunition.

A round big hole right into the darkness of your brain. White at the end of it. Lumps, torn lumps, around it. Also all yellow. Horror made wound. Never ever to be cancelled from one's eyes. One of the many tickets for hatred and revenge. How much life can one give now, to get at the source of that horror made wound? Wipe it from the face of the Earth.

Between the centre blocks of flats and the block which faces Rossville Street, there is another corner, another passage to the courtyard, a telephone box. And here it is like before, at the corner after Chamberlain Street. Everybody pressed into and around the telephone box. No safety yet. Bang-kchhhh, bang-kchhhh, bang-kchhhh... From the walls and from the little barricade across the road, where Saracens are eyeing and spitting. Bullets from behind armoured plates into open layers of soft life, to make big holes, to make life run from them. Good training, mad scientists. Great stuff... "Our boys." The best Army in the world!

I recognise known faces. Friends. The boy with glasses and red hair, straight out from *Lord of the Flies*. A boy. An Irish boy. A son of a mother and a father. A boy who plays and wants to do great, beautiful, good things. Like all boys upon whom the mad scientists haven't laid hands yet. A boy of the human race. Now close to death. Inexplicable, crazy death. Why should I die, die and get so horribly yellow? I haven't done anything. My mother loves me. My friends play with me. I haven't done anything yet. His eyes are small behind the glasses. Small and red. And his face seems to have become smaller. He looks at me. Shakes his head and looks for a long time. Can you tell me why? You come from far away. Perhaps you know those insects, all things, better, and understand them. Better than us, behind our barricades in our tiny, free city.

There was a commotion when I came down from McGuigan, my eyes full of yellow. A few people had gone towards the corner of the building. A man (1) lies there now. He looks like the first in the row, Doherty. But he is another one. Another dead. Was coming round the corner. Running from Rossville street a few seconds ago. Got hit in the back as he was reaching out for the door handle of the entrance, just before the corner. Clutched his belly where the bullet had come through. Staggered on, past the entrance, round the corner, reached out towards people at the corner, people stretched out their hands to hold him up, pulled him away, fell, was dead. Close to him, the banner of the Civil Rights march.

CIVIL RIGHTS, white on blue. Red on white on blue. Untidy stains, as if a bucket had been thrown over it. Blood all over, like an explosion. Like those paintings made by monkeys. Blood and bits of human matter. And around Gilmore, more, bigger parts, wet, slimy, red, grey, parts of human matter. Like in a butchery. Entrails here, carcass there.

Still shots being fired. Same sound, same bullets, same guns. SLR guns. Made to

(1) Hugh Gilmore, 17 years.

kill. To kill even elephants. And the sound gets monotonous. Isn't heard any more, becomes normal. People move away from hiding places, covers, shelters, doors, telephone boxes, niches in walls. Look for things to do, immediately, to feel still alive in all the death. Nurse the hopeless bodies, first aid men and girls among them, red eyes, tears in their eyes, working professionally, pedantically, not giving a damn about themselves. The bravest people in the world. In front and under the guns, under the narrow, masked gaze of insects, the greatest cowards in the world.

A girl breaks down, slumps along the wall, and cries softly, then louder, then screams her head off. Long, wailing. She had seen Gilmore's eyes. She had heard: "Don't let me die alone... " And she hadn't been able to move. Two nurses, a first aid boy, other men and boys hurry to her aid. Lift her gently, she sinks back into somebody's lap, and screams, screams. More chilling than anything before. The sudden realisation of horror, death, horrific mass-death. So-called humanity gone primeval, back to savagery. What will it do to you when you wake up to the realisation? She is caressed, softly talked to, comforted. She relents, the wail ebbs slowly away. Everybody has tears in their eyes, but doesn't mind them. Probably don't even know they are there. Operates. Two boys, their pal just shot out of his and their lives, have their arms round each other and walk slowly by, slowly, weeping. Susan stands in front of them, microphone limp along her side. One boy puts his head on her shoulder. She strokes his hair, gently. Wide open eyes of Susan, wide and dry. Too many tears to find a way out. Before, when I was going past the dead bodies and the lying, crawling, living. I had turned back and had seen, to the freezing of my blood, Susan coming down behind me, in the open, without cover, waving a little white hankie. Wanting to do, not knowing what to do. Not bearing to be out of it, on the sideline, a reporter. Suffocating at the thought that others should think her not part of them. I know. And I had screamed at her to get to the wall, leaving her dazed and uncertain. Others had called her in, among them. Now she was near me again.

At the small rubble barricade across the road two bodies were lying(1). Young bodies, small, it seemed. A man came from yet another huddle of fright behind the Free Derry side of the building on the other end of the barricade, towards Glenfada Park. He looked straight at us. Not at paratroopers and Saracens just a few yards away. He had his hands crossed over his head. He walked firmly, not hurriedly. We were holding our breath, this side of the street. Bang-kchhhh... . The man fell. He staggered, on his knees, towards one of the small bodies felled before, spread slack over the rubble. He touched the body. He raised his hand. Truce, mercy. Decency. You must. It's enough now.

It isn't. More shots, from very near, straight at the group of this man, broken in two, and a slack, uncoordinated body at his feet. The man is hit. Also the small body jerks, hit again, while dead. Or still dying? It's the broken in two man's young son.

Reactions get going again. First preoccupation: the dimension of the horror, the extent of the losses.

"I saw three dead behind the flats, and three here."

"There are more dead over there, at Glenfada Park."

"They killed two at the barricade."

"In William Street too. Somebody saw three bodies thrown into a Saracen, like dead meat."

"I saw them catching some lads and beating them into the Saracens with the butt of the carbines."

"Over there, at Glenfada, the whole place is full of bodies. I just came over. A massacre."

"Watch out, the massacre is still going on. The bastards aren't happy yet. They want to kill us all."

The girl of before starts screaming again. The volume of the buzzing noise

(1) William Nash, 19 years,
John Young, 17 years.

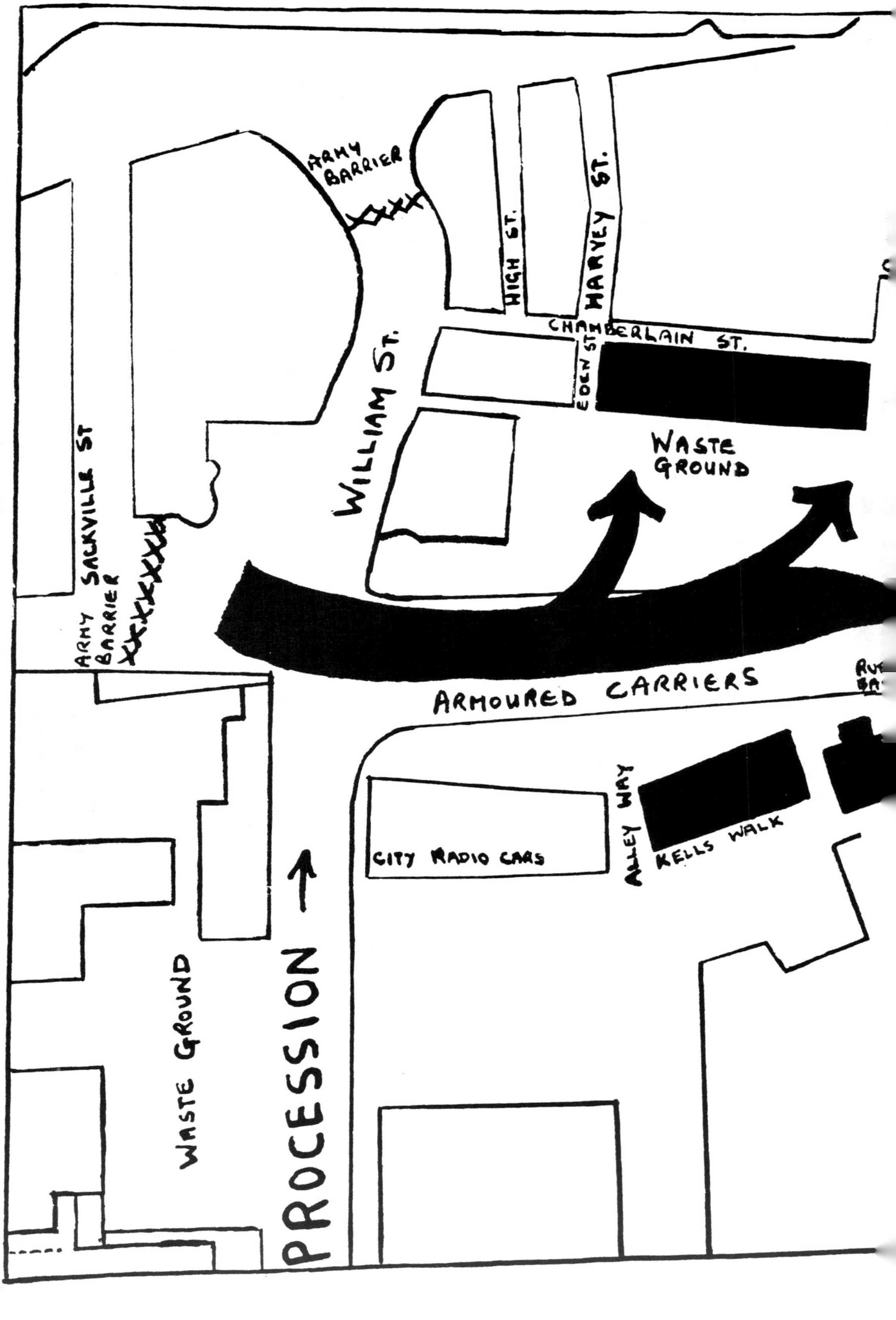
ARMY BARRIER
HIGH ST.
HARVEY ST.
CHAMBERLAIN ST.
EDEN ST
WILLIAM ST.
WASTE GROUND
SACKVILLE ST
ARMY BARRIER
ARMOURED CARRIERS
ALLEY WAY
KELLS WALK
CITY RADIO CARS
PROCESSION
WASTE GROUND

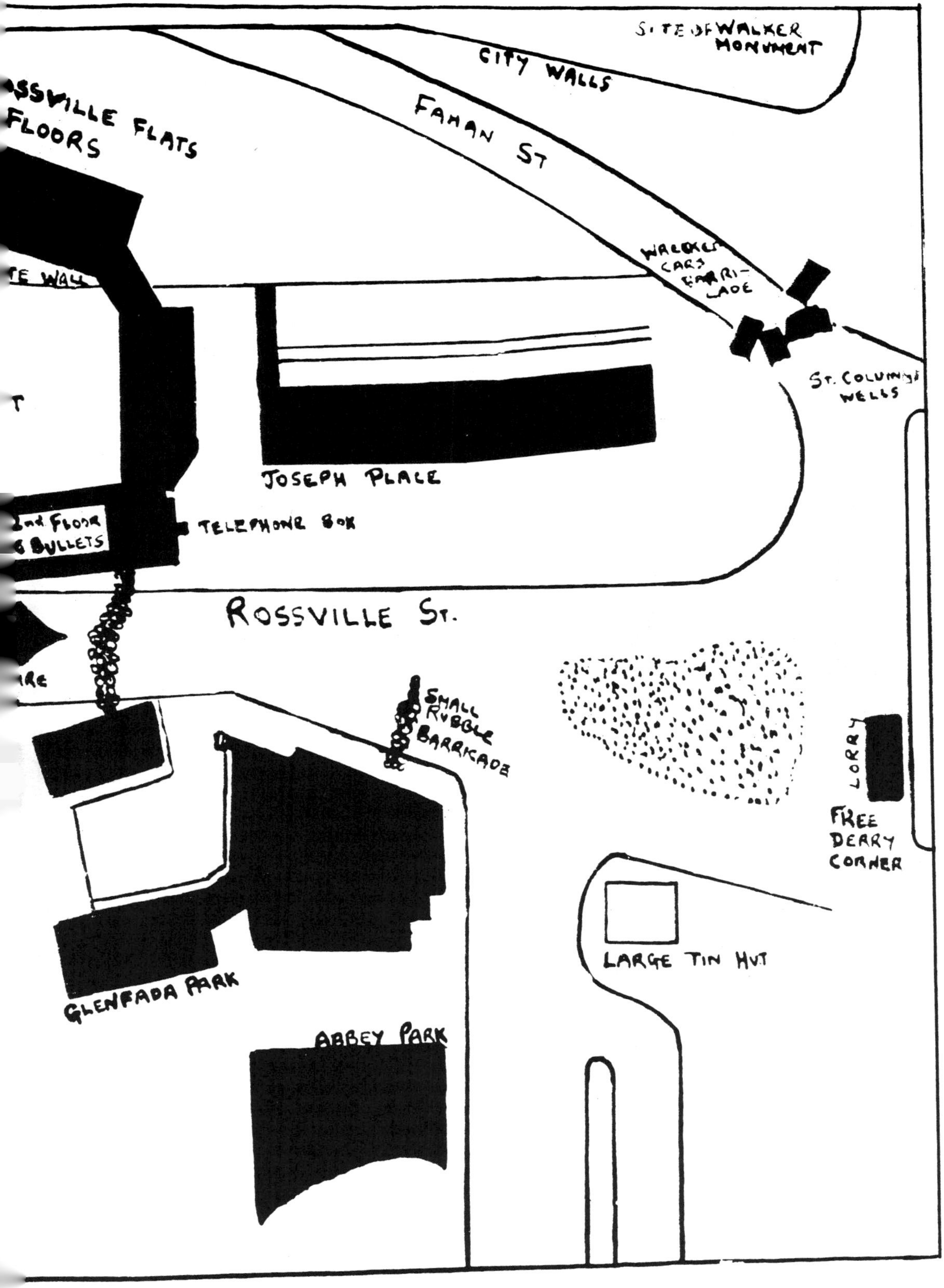
SITE OF WALKER MONUMENT
CITY WALLS
FAHAN ST
FLOORS
WRECKED CARS BARRICADE
ST. COLUMB'S WELLS
JOSEPH PLACE
TELEPHONE BOX
ROSSVILLE ST.
SMALL RUBBLE BARRICADE
LORRY
FREE DERRY CORNER
LARGE TIN HUT
GLENFADA PARK
ABBEY PARK

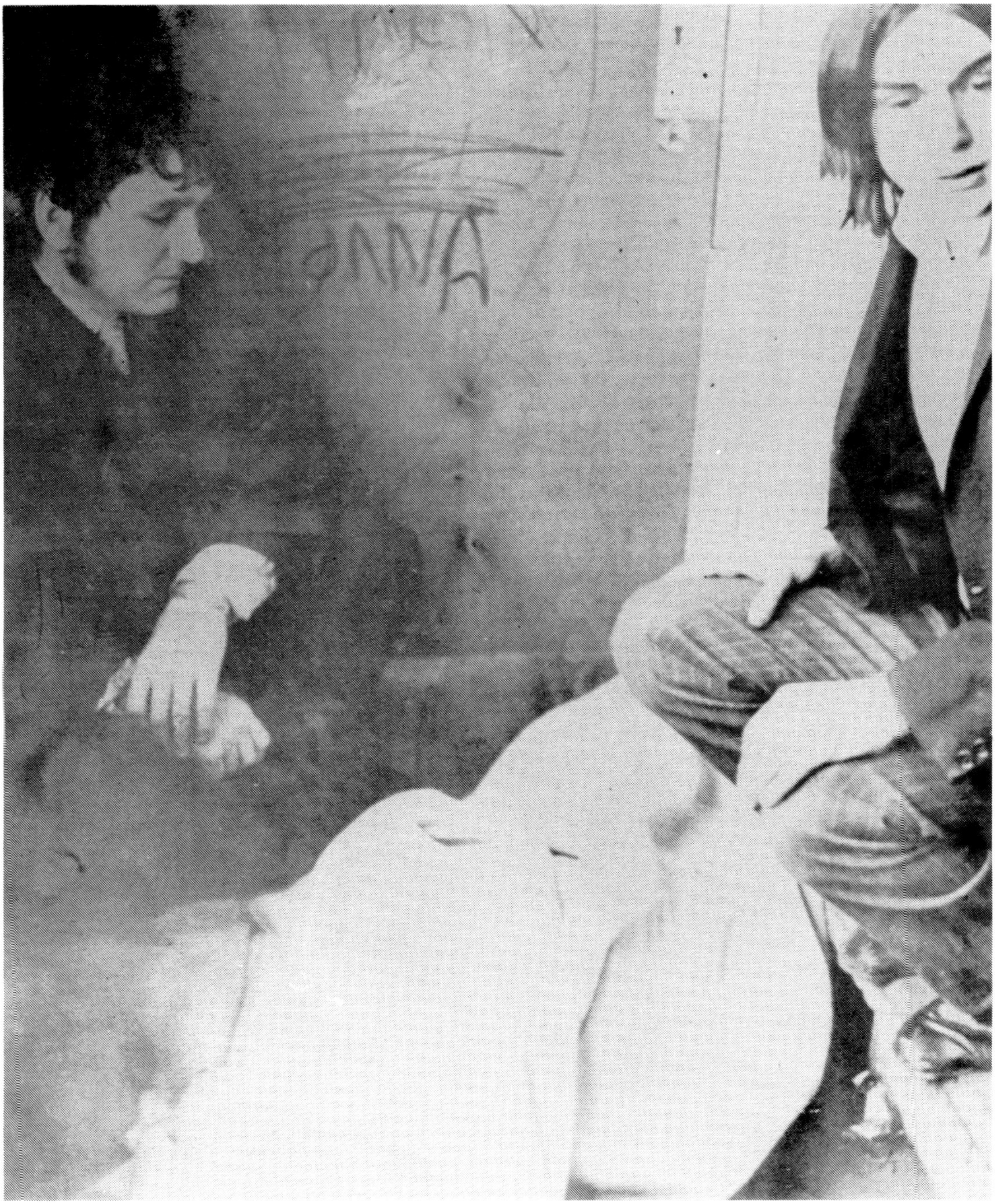

another body, covered with a yellow cloth... on the landing... At both sides... young boys...

The Saracens... back at the beginning of the building...
One with a red cross on top.

rises again. Gets articulated. Renewed shouts, curses. Bastards. BASTARDS.

From behind the corner, straight into the small, vicious hole of the guns. Pandemonium. The extent of what is happening starts sinking in. Too much for many. And if now they come in and mow us down, all of us? They are shooting anybody. Always in the back. I heard some, laughing and jumping around like bloody maniacs. It must be about eight dead. No, it's at least ten. Ten so far. What about the boys? What boys? The IRA, aren't they going to do something, to stop the pigs? Better if they stay out. The bastards don't want anything better: IRA coming out, them coming in, with 500 Saracens and thousands of paratroopers. If they try and move on, over the barricades, then it's time for the IRA... Christ, if I only had a gun, a gun, a gun... Christ. Where is Charlie? Nobody saw Charlie? I think he was down, with the others, at the meeting. I got to find my sister. Thirteen years old and as thick as mud. Would walk straight into it. What, what can we do with stones?

Drop that stone, lad, if they see you with it, they'll get you. Better if we all move back to the Inn, they won't dare come in there. I stay here. This is our first barricade. They are not coming over here. They may, if they think everybody's gone. They might even think there are some of us with guns here... Might hold them off.

KILL THE REPORTER

I want to telephone. The hell knows whom. Anybody with sense, out of this madhouse. Anybody who may stop it, or at least scream it out into the world, to stop it. I used to work for that Roman daily years ago. They might be able to do something. Contact the government, tell them to tell the British Embassy, the United Nations, the hell. Stupid. But what else? There must be some sense left, somewhere. I slide round the corner with Rossville Street, with Susan. There is an entrance to the flat, in front of the barricade. Ten yards from the first Saracen. And on the first floor that woman we met last time we were here. She's got a telephone. We make it round the corner and into the entrance. More people here. Can't move. Outside the door is death. Huddled in dark corners, arms crossed, shrinking into the back, trembling. At the end of the first flight of steps, blood coming down in a trickle, from step to step. Somebody wounded, perhaps, who got into a home. No, another body, covered with a yellow cloth. Yellow is death, forever. Right on the landing, occupying the whole of the landing. Shoes and turnovers sticking out from under the yellow sheet. At both sides, sitting, squatting, young boys, chins on their hands, silent. What's the matter with him? Large, dark eyes on us: "He is dead." Large, dark eyes still on us. A long, long time. Perhaps they can understand death if they read it on our faces.

Long, difficult step over the covered mass. Through the sitting boys. And up again, to the first floor. The entrance to the woman's flat is four or five doors down a balcony opening and looking onto Rossville courtyard. Where the butchery started. Where the steel boxes still sit, silent now. Horrific. The balcony is deserted. Anybody appearing on it can come under fire from below. Rifles and trunks are pointed here too. We lift our hands over our heads and push on. No stopping now. All those deaths have really made us immune from fear. All those deaths and a purpose. Keep going.

That woman won't let anybody in. They whisper this from a narrow gap in the next door. And shake their heads. They mean: she is different from us all. Us that can be killed, massacred, but not deprived of our love for each other, of our being part of all the others, of being human. In front of this door, a bucket of water and a roll of paper tissues. Against the gas, for whoever needs it.

I bang against the door as if I was about to knock it down. And would have done. The woman peeps through a window, recognises us, opens, lets us in. Diving on the phone in the bedroom, which has the window on Rossville Street. Operator, operator, operator, operator quick. Rome... The man on the other side sounds normal. NORMAL. Hasn't he heard the bangs, the screams, hasn't he seen the monsters, smelled the blood, isn't yellow all over his eyes? "Take it easy, what is your number... what is it you want...? I'll try Rome." Try? You must give me Rome, now. Now. Operator, operator... Waiting for the call, I go near the window. There are children in the house. Some TV set is blaring out firm, crazily normal voices. Orange juice, cornflakes, margarine. A girl of about 12 appears like a ghost in the bedroom door. Mouth wide open. Uncomprehending. In the room, around this huge bed that occupies the whole place, the woman and Susan. What happened? They are murdering everybody, that's what happened.

From the window I can see from the beginning of the block, at the small barricade, to the entrance of Rossville Street from William Street. An ambulance has arrived near the barricade, white men pick up bodies like berries from the rubble. A little crowd is at the backdoor of the ambulance and helps.

The Saracens, with a few insects floating around them, are now back at the beginning of the building. Two or three of them. One with a red cross on top. For insects hurt by fleeing humans with nothing but sweat in their hands.

I take a picture, two, three... Somebody from the Saracens moves forward. Better not to be seen up here. I withdraw and turn to the women. Then, fantastically loud, bang-kchhhh... crash. I see a hole as big as ten-pence in the glass. My eye hurts, like full of sand. Splinters. The woman runs out and up the stairs. DOWN! I on top of Susan. Pull a chair behind us.

Bang-kchhhh-crash... bang-kchhhh-crash... bang-kchhhh-crash... bang-kchhhh-crash... bang-kchhhh-crash... Five times. Five ten pence holes in the window, all over it, in perfect symmetry. Well trained insects. We crawl away, towards the hall, lay still. That was narrow. Just around our heads. "Shall I keep recording?" Only if there is noise.

Susan crawls on. Head down, for Christ's sake, flat on your belly. Up the stairs. Tell everybody to move towards the back of the flat, away from the front windows. Children screaming. The woman goes hysteric; that was at you, for taking photos, that was at you, for taking photos. Eight times, platinum blonde bleached hair, sweating forehead, bulging eyes appearing over the railing of the stairs, for a second, yelling. Yelling on, other things, to the children, who have started crying. Susan, short-breathed but warmly: "You must get away from that window, come here, to the back, slowly, don't get up, try and wriggle like a snake. Stay down." To the children. The crying dies down. One can hear the TV again. A commercial for the Army: Good pay, quick promotion, see the world. Emphatic. Persuasively melodical. Almost triumphant. Reassuring. Voice from a fat belly, from a contented mind. Fed on innocent blood. The mad scientist spreading honey for the insects, to get them, put masks with trunks on them, paint them black and send them out to murder. For he is a vampire and needs good, warm, strong blood to survive.

Then another sound comes through, from Rome.

I wriggle, fish for the receiver. The voice comes from the Moon, from somewhere in empty space. "Hey, how are you?" "The British are massacring the people here..." "How interesting... got a story?" "The hell!... tell somebody... get some bum high up... " No understanding; no communication. I leave Rome in its empty space.

We must get out of here. If they are after us, because of the pictures and what we may say, they now know where we are and they'll come and get us. Elephant bullets like those through the window, splashed into the whole place. No getting away. For nobody. But, getting out? Probably those who shot have now radioed our position to the Saracens in the courtyard, who may watch the front door and as soon as we get out... "Phone the army", screams the woman. "Tell them that you are only taking photos, or they'll shoot you as you get out." They know, alright. They know that we take photos and recordings telling true stories. Weren't they after us before? They don't like it.

Bang-kchhhh-crash... five times... see a hole as big as tenpence in the glass.

They kill to stop unfriendly, truthful photos. They wanted to kill some weeks ago, when they saw us here, among the people. Gave the order through army radio. They chased us with pointed guns at the Long Kesh march, at Republican funerals, as we were pointing the lens on their flat faces. And, as we slipped away among the people, our people, contented themselves with spitting and cursing the people.

"You must phone the Army, to have them repair the window, tell them that I am not doing anything!... You must phone..."

Still, we got to get out of this trap. Crawl to the door, open it, get out normally and swiftly, put Susan on the side of the wall, hands up, over the head, glimpse down at the murderers, move on feeling some slight itching down the back, wanting to run, steady, steady, the door to the landing. Out.

At the main entrance somebody comes running up. "Did you hear the Army radio? Was saying that there was a photographer taking pictures behind a window in Rossville Flats... "

There, at the back of the High Flats again, in Joseph Place. Quiet now. Normal voices, only slightly anxious. Still counting the dead. Twelve, eighteen, fifteen? So many wounded. A woman has had a heart attack and has died. So many boys taken away. It must be around 4.40. Light fading. From the vividness of before, slowly normal colours re-emerging, on faces and things. Gilles, a French photographer, is there. Taking pictures like a robot, of blood puddles, rests of humans, the bodies have been removed, stained Civil Rights banner. His face is longer and thinner, unshaven. He was clean shaven an hour ago. His eyes are all over the face. Mumbles unconnected things. Looks me in the face as if he didn't recognise me. Keeps clicking away, stops, looks around with a blank expression of terror. Out of his mind.

Now I remember. Out of the fuzz of shooting, falling, running, twisting, spluttering, screaming, bleeding, banging, his thin figure emerges. He was heading towards a fallen body. Hands high above his head, cameras dangling from his neck, shouting "Press, Press"... A paratrooper laying on, straight at him, he seeing it, leaping through the air, landing hard on his belly, the paratrooper firing three times over him, from ten yards, then having finished his magazine not being able to shoot any more and Gilles drifting away into the tossing mass, into memory. Not a good time for murderous insect photographing photographers today.

Annoy the mad scientist. Bother his computerised plan. The unforeseen grain of truth getting into the prettily decorated murder machine, tearing a bit of pretty cover off, exposing the hallucinated eye of Satan...

THE CURSE OF THE DEAD GENERATIONS AND OF ALL GENERATIONS TO COME...

Five o'clock. It's getting dark. The event has taken place. The mass execution of thirteen people, the hurting and maiming of another sixteen have been successfully accomplished. Punishment has been effectively meted out by a swarm of excellently trained, programmed, conditioned insects. Small, black, poisonous, with trunks. Filthy flies, good only to spit death on behalf of their scared-to-death scientists.

Mad, power-mad scientists. Vampires devoid of life of their own, now bulging and bouncing with strong, good people's blood, in candid shirts, impeccable suits, neat ties, shiny cheeks, well rounded mouths, monster paws and monster fangs drawn in, monster face made up. Back to Dr Jekyll, high with innocent, good, strong people's blood, ready to face the world in the time proven cloak of justice, law, order, in the tissue of lie, in the frock of hypocrisy, drawn over the putrefying flesh that feeds poisonous insects.

Under the shadow slowly pouring down, figures standing motionless in the scenery of murder and martyrdom. Hands in their pockets. Hands clutched round chests, eyes away from it all, up the hill, beyond Creggan. Beyond everything. In total silence. Erect. Composed. Minutes of silence in the faint light that flickers from the tricoloured flag on the pole beside the barricade. Unordered. Minutes of silence, putting to shame all "minutes of silence" anywhere, at any time, under any flag.

Then the figures slowly start moving again. And speaking, quietly, normally. Realisation not too hard to come by, in people used to horror for three years, for fifty years, for centuries. In people who knew the price demanded for the refusal of slavery, exploitation, submission, sweat and hunger and chains, for the refusal of their strong, good blood.

The main effort is to turn the irrational, mad dimension of horror into numbers, an assessment of losses, a measure of how much the community has suffered. A habit of people who's life is fight and will always be, till liberation. Out of the lists of dead and wounded and disappeared, the embryo of history emerges. Of true history, not cover-up history to cover up their living off the blood of others, but history of your own blood, that cannot lie, has no need to lie. And one can see why these things produce IRA, victory. Because they produce togetherness, closeness, understanding of who and what the enemy really is, force. They feed the monster for minutes, hours, days perhaps. But they make togetherness, Sinn Féin, IRA, Revolution, for ever.

Names emerge. And the pain grows specific, localised, somewhere around the heart, or the stomach, or the lungs. Everybody knew — and, here, knowing means loving — someone among the fallen, the hurt. Us too. We are part of the people. And this is what makes us and what we write, indisputable, impartial, objective.

The pavement bleeds. Shadows fall upon puddles and rests of human life. Turn them into water and dust and rubble. Into earth. A new start from a stronger earth. A few hundred yards away, beyond the skyline of William Street, under the watchtowers with their eyes of stupidity and hate, troopers fester upon recollections of cowardice, munch glorious memories of savagery, blood dripping from their black, poisonous trunks. The air is still pungent with mustardy gas-breath. Only now we feel it again.

Death had happened amongst us. But only now it flows slowly into the city, tosses around doorsteps, filters into rooms, drowns homes, chokes people. A small house in the road that goes from the Bogside up, towards Creggan. Any house. A mother, her children. She sits in an armchair, torn by age and poverty. The story of Derry, of Ireland, of the ordinary people under slavery and in the will of freedom, engraved in her face, sculptured in her bones. In '69 the onslaught of the vampires gave her a stroke. She is paralysed from the waist down. She weeps and screams. Everybody in here has had something precious amputated by the filthy insects' sting, burned away, reduced into ashes: a friend, a cousin, a sister-in-law, a warm face of daily life. And the coalesced pain is unbearable.

The woman screams, trying to tear away from her poor, dead limbs, shaking wildly from side to side, silver hair flying, strains of grey, and all the grey surges up again. And then the yellow, yellower, Doherty, Kevin, McGuigan, Gilmore, Nash, Duddy... yellower. God, how horrible.

Pressed against the corner of the couch, all on his own, a lad of perhaps sixteen sits, legs crossed, desperately trying to pull together, arms crossed to squeeze all his strength to himself, weeping quietly. He weeps and weeps. And doesn't move. Moving, losing composure, would probably mean screaming too, sobbing, going mad.

And the old woman screams. "They have killed that wee lad's pal. They have killed his pal, poor lad. They... they... MURDERERS... they are murderers... " Girls, young sons around her. Tears flowing, eyes drowned, faces tossed to the ceiling not to give in to the madness, placating, caressing. "Please mum, please... please mummy... mummy... please..."

The woman screams. Sees in. Pain that destroys coordination and rationality gets under control, becomes articulated, articulates causes and effects and, thus, struggle. Struggle this people know. Everything they turn into struggle. Beaten down, maimed, paralysed, with a mountain of horror on their back, with an ocean of pain in their hearts, they struggle. And the woman looks at us and screams: "Tell the world, tell about the murderers, we hate them. Hate them. Tell the Pope, tell Lynch. No good... Lynch is no good. He lets his people be butchered up here. No good. Tell him." And then, surging upwards, limbs vitalised by strength of spirit. "WE SHALL NOT SURRENDER. WE SHALL NOT FORGIVE, NEVER. THE CURSE OF THE DEAD GENERATIONS ON THE MURDERERS, OF THE DEAD GENERATIONS, THE CURSE OF THE DEAD GENERATIONS AND OF ALL THE GENERATIONS TO COME. THEY WON'T GET US NEVER. And they will not beat us, the murderers, with their Common Market and their robberies, all their robberies, all their tricks, their killings. We will wreck that Common Market, double-crossers, wreck it... "

"Tell Lynch, tell Hume. NEVER. CURSE... CURSE, THE CURSE OF EVERY IRISHMAN..."

In the house where the boys are, the boys who defend Free Derry, only swift movements, in and out of rooms, gangways, front doors, stringent words softly and firmly spoken, rapid consultations, telephone calls, concentration, organisation. Total reaction. Under total control. Total absence of the irrational. Emotional under the unbreakable control of militancy and duty. Pale, grave faces, but enlivened by intent, action, purpose. We are sitting in front of the fire, us and a few others, girls, who come in to warm up briefly. One brings soup for everybody. Few have time or desire for soup. We wait till somebody gets us away, from Free Derry to some phoney free communication channel with the world. Free only because of selfish interest and calculation. Free only so that blood goes to another set of mad vampires. Vampires kill each other, not to look into the face of their own death.

And there are rumours that the British are stopping all reporters and photographers leaving Free Derry, and taking away their material. Six o'clock. On TV, BBC news. The tottering face of a pinky cannibal in the same uniform of the insects, plus some more grotesque stripes and spots. Stands on the spot of the massacre. Stench of murder around his fat feet and his pinky, stupid face. Does his part in the service of the vampires. Mini-vampire in insect uniform. The stop-gap, to keep the mad scientist-vampires credible and effective with the insects.

"My men have only fired three rounds... after being fired at and have had nailbombs, petrol-bombs and other ugly things thrown at them... " The stage for the poor dears, for "our magnificent boys enduring death and injury in their peace-keeping role in Ireland", is set.

Embellishing little stitching on the rot covering cloak of the vampires. The ready-made headline to whip money, endless piles of money, out of ignorance and into the pockets of the vampire-addicted printing insects: Daily Mirror, BBC, ITV, Guardian, The Times, Daily Mail, Daily Express, The Financial Times... The Sun, Evening News, Evening Standard... Each a little paper boat for vampires, to float over seas of blood and dip in, here and there...

As General Ford says: "Three rounds... " I hold in my hands, in front of the TV set, 43 empty SLR cartridges, brand new, fresh from the barrel, and a dozen bullets picked from walls and flesh. Ford, you are a mean, stupid, disgusting, grotesque, dirty liar... And now, Ford... murderer Ford, come and get us. Use another few of your bullets on us. Or do you prefer your bold paratroopers to capture us, hold us out to you, so that you can amuse yourself longer? Plucking and tearing and burning with your Benson cigarette-ends? Electrocute my genitals? Scream the noise of the machine that governs you into my ear and brain?... put hoods on us so that we forget that we belong to this people?... drop us from some helicopter?... baton us; lock us into freeze and fright?... pull us out again; tear us apart, jump on us with your tiny fat feet? ... hop up and down on our faces; crunch us, smash us, cancel us...? In your customary way...

We leave at midnight. Fool the British. Get away. Drive all night, with the boys. In silence. Sickness in the throat. Torn, tattered, sound and strong flesh under the eyelids. Along the icy roads. South... To give the world some yellow...

And to shout across the earth:
"DERRY IS FREE!"

A F T E R M A T H

AT HOME

1st Daughter: This young boy's friend shot dead. An old man of sixty shot dead. So many young boys slaughtered. A child shot dead under its father's eyes...

Mother: Tell them what the British Army has done. Tell them... (screams, sobs)... Tell the world...

Daughters and son (weeping): Mummy... mummy.

Mother: Tell the world, it must go round the world. Tell them what bastards the British Army are. Tell them what they do to our people... And tell the Dublin Government too.

Daughters and son: Mummy... mummy calm down... mummy sit down please...

Mother: And tell the Dublin Government that they are no good. They are watching their own Irish people getting slaughtered (screams and screams). Dublin is no good...

Daughters and son: Mummy, for heaven's sake be quiet, please... mummy...

Mother: Tell them that the people of Ireland have had enough, hundreds of years...

2nd daughter: Oh God, she is killing herself...

Mother: Everybody shot at today... People marching for their civil rights and being shot down... Cancerous, treacherous rats. And we'll shoot the soldiers down, every one of them. Because the Protestants said that they would stop us and shoot at us. They have done it (sobbing, convulsions, screams).

Son: They'll pay for it, they'll pay for it...

Mother (trying to rise on her paralysed feet): God's curse on them, and the curse of the dead generations of Irish (voice reaches a pitch, long wailing scream)... the curse of the dead generations of Irish, the Irish masses, they have taken Irish life...

Daughters: Mummy, be good. Mummy...

Mother: ...And the curse of every Irish man upon them... the curse of every Irish man... (pandemonium in the room, only the small boy on the settee weeps quietly away, staring in front of him, legs crossed, all wrapped up in himself)... Tell the Pope... tell the...

1st daughter: Mummy, don't be saying anything against the Pope...

Mother: Tell him, tell him... Let me say it...

(I tell the woman to be calm, not to upset herself and her children, to try and be strong. She quietens down a little, makes a visible effort of self-control, slumps back into her armchair. Low sobbing everywhere in the room. Heavy panting of the woman.)

2nd Daughter: They shot him... as he was running. They shot three dead...

Son: They shot three dead beside me...

2nd Daughter: And they pushed a poor young fellow against a wall and shot him...

Mother: ... poor young fellow against the wall and shot him DEAD (raises her voice again into a scream). They shot that wee boy's pal here... seventeen... them bastards (her words are drowned in crying).

Son: Mummy you get sick...

2nd Daughter: Mummy, stop it...

1st Daughter: She can't help it. You know she can't help it... (the woman's screams and crying makes everything else incomprehensible).

Mother (now slightly calmer, firm): And that con of the Common Market. We don't want them near us. And when they get in it they'll wreck Germany and they'll wreck the Dutch and they were double-dealers all their life. They're the worst race in the world for double dealing. When they get into the Common Market they'll wreck it, and I hope they do wreck it. So that everybody steps from them...

2nd Daughter: Mummy... (pleading) Mummy control yourself...

Mother: Don't get us into the press, Mister... don't quote my name...

Son: ... and this boy was shot in the back...

1st Daughter: Don't quote our names...

2nd Daughter: They shot at the Priest...

Voice: They shot at the Priest when he went to give him the last rites, they shot at him, he had to crouch, did you see that?

Mother: Don't quote our names, Mister. You'll get us all interned. They'll shoot every one of us...

Susan: You were lucky to get away, weren't you?

Mother: We were all lucky to get away. Me son, me daughter, me mother-in-law... my brother-in-law when he took a fellow to the ambulance, to help together, and my brother-in-law and they took the boy dying... There were three dead bodies laying down at the barricade, they wouldn't even let the priest onto them... (screaming again)... Quote all that in your papers. We're telling the truth. They are telling the lies...

Susan: Yes, we saw it this afternoon...

1st Daughter: You must hide your films...

Mother: You'll not get out of Derry with them tonight... You'll not...

1st Daughter: You better watch it you don't come under a raid tonight and they take 'em off you tonight... you better hide them... somewhere...

Son: They shot this man Mac...

2nd Daughter: (he had the) films of all the rioting... they shot him... he was running...

Mother: And there was no ricochet bullet... never...

2nd Daughter: ... shooting and he actually dropping on the ground. Dead... and the Army say he was shot by a ricochetting bullet in the back of the head...

Mother: A man that was religious, holy, you know one of these men, he wouldn't cross his hands, like... if he thought it was wrong... There he was coming over the barricade and they aimed a bullet... and they shot him DEAD. A man, a religious... he would have thought it a crime... these murderers... they shot him dead...

Susan: Do you think they'll come into Creggan tonight?

Mother: Aye, they'll come in... they'll come in... they'll come in... they terrorise us night after night...

Son: ... I don't know how many dead... You hide your films...

Mother: ... If they thought you had them...

1st Daughter: They censor the British Press...

Mother: Don't forget... Telefis Éireann, for that's heavily censored too... that's heavily censored too. (They are all around the wailing mother, weeping, speaking softly and tenderly to her. Stroking her head. The young boy still sits against the corner of the divan and weeps quietly, staring in front of himself, at the face of his dead pal.)

<u>In the home of William Nash, 19 years old, murdered.</u>

The mother of William has a severe heart condition and was released from hospital three days after the massacre. The father was wounded in the arm and chest when he tried to aid his son.

Son: Mother came out of hospital just now...

Mother (sobbing, her voice trailing away and turning into a cry): I didn't know that they'd shot him... I read it in the paper the next morning. One of the wee nurses, one of the new wee nurses came up with a paper the next morning... that's when I knew what happened (her voice breaks)...

Voice: You're lucky that you still have your husband. I saw him crossing the road and being shot at...

Mother: My son meant more to me than my husband (weeps)... my son meant more to me... Everything I touch... wherever I turn my head ... there is something reminding me of him (constant low murmur in the background, women trying to find words of comfort)... And then Martin told me... And then I looked and saw that wee boy Duddy (first murdered) saw a whole lot of them and they clubbed together... the wee boy Gilmore and all... I'll never get over it (sobs heavily, shrinks into the back of her armchair, her voice getting thinner and thinner)... I can't get through this again... not yet... I just can't (breaks completely down. Is helped out of her chair and into another room. Sobs quietly)... Excuse me, please...

Father: My boy, he's never done nothing in his life. You've seen me at that barricade, where I ran over to get him, and I put my hands up, like that, up there, and they gave it to me there and there (indicates wounds on arm and chest). That's the truth, that's what happened, I'm telling you. Not one of them had a nail bomb... You know it... I know it. See... them youngsters all shot, murdered, as I say... I... I... I gave them statements alright. But you see, you have to give it the right way... they were murdered and you know it. So do I. Willy, you see, Willy, the son of mine, he may have fired a stone. OK, so what? Stones is nothing. I even see him firing it, but, probably, maybe he was there. I am not saying he never fired stones, probably he did fire stones... they are firing stones down there now. They fired gas into... they say they were fired at. But they are saying now that they are being fired at from the Cathedral, rifles from the Cathedral, and they are firing across Glenfada Park, gas, so much gas, thousands, and they say two or three, and just now live bullets, tracer bullets down the road.

And you see that gas, you know it, see that gas... see the first time the gas came in, the first time they threw gas it was easy, just a hankie to protect you. Now, no chance. See, once you get it you're finished...

Son: You know, between me and my brother we have 18 years of British Army between us. I was there till two months ago and my brother, he was nine years with the Army and my father's father, he was decorated in two World Wars, and my mother's father, he was decorated in two World Wars too, we were far from being nationalist...

Father: I tell you the whole story. I tell you the truth. I left here at about eleven o'clock. Right? I motored down. It cost me about 25 minutes to get me down, into town. And I went into a bar, you know, for a drink. Right? It might have been quarter past two when I came out. Had a few stouts. That's nothing. It's easy for a drinker that, isn't it? Because of no money, you know... I could have drunk more, if I had it. And this friend of mine says we'll get a taxi up home. But, ach, no taxi. So we walked through the cemetery, right down. The march started to take off and that was about three o'clock. Near enough. I got into the march... I lost my friend. So we got down to William Street, you know, the TV Flats. I got down, anyway. You know the water cannon. I got drowned then.

Another son of mine came down to look for me. He told me that this missus had come from England, for his mother. You know, she is not very well at all. He said he'd go and look for my boy. And he went. So I got a bit browned off, you know, you know when you get sick, all that gas. So I went across the street. You know, that wee barricade? This didn't happen then... I walked across the street at the wee barricade, there, you know, the wee flats, Glenfada Park. So I was going across, you know, when you heard banging... (voice descends to a whisper)... I looked round... you know the shooting...

and I looked round and I saw the wee fellow of mine... I say that's Willy... and I've seen... So, as fast as I could get over, I run like... I run across. There is some banging then, you see. I run across the street then, you know, to get Willy. But I knew ... that he was gone... I knew it... I knew it. And I put my hand up like that... as I put my hand up there, they give it to me in here and then here... two like, two, aye. See, when I jumped down like that, they kept on pumping at me, you see. So that was alright.

I've seen Willy... the young fellow was there... while I was there... my own body was laying there... three bodies laying there... like that. He got it in the temple. Willy was in the middle, the son of mine, you see. He was laying face down, but his face was laying out that way... but there was no breath coming out. So I touched him and I said "Willy", like that, there... and they kept pumping... and I got him like that there... and I had him like that there... his shirt was right up, you know, he's a right big fellow, isn't he, he's pretty big for his age... and I just touched him like that and I said "Willy". And I couldn't do nothing for him...

Another wee fellow, on the other side of him, he was dead. Three dead. So that was alright. A big Saracen tank there, and I kept low... See, the street was all panic, and then we were away, so, what I know, what I heard after, see, that soldier... he came down mad, at that Finnegan Park, and he fired, that's where that other man, what do you call him, was shot in the head. McGuigan, he fired point blank and got him there... shot him cold dead. When I walked across the street he was just laying out. Do you see...

I walked across the street? Did you mind that priest, he had a wee word with me, he did this for me there. I don't know if you've seen that or not. He saw the three bodies over there. He couldn't go over (he raises his voice)... See, if he went across the street, to examine them, to give them a wee bit of prayer, or something like that, they would have shot him. Oh, aye, they would have shot him dead, that's why he COULDN'T go over. But he said, he told me "I couldn't go over", because they'd shoot him.

What happened when the Saracen tank came up, that's what I'm telling you now. Saracen tank came driving up, like a tank, and the two boys jumped out, and what did he say? "Three more dead bodies"... As God may strike me stiff stone dead... I'll never forget that... I thought they were going to shoot me, you see. I was wounded, you see, they knew I was wounded, seen the blood pumping out of me. I thought they'd finish me off there and then, you see. But this boy (soldier) said, they just left me sitting, "three more bodies"... and I say to this big fella, I say "see, that's my son there"... Just dragged them in the dirt... one boy on top of the others... I thought they were going to finish me. But then he ran across the street, with another soldier... he was murdering the crowd... that's when McGuigan got it... that's when he got it. But when I walked across the street, there were three more dead bodies, I thought they'd finish me off. But the big Saracen tank took away and left me there and I got up like that. And I walked across the street. But see, this man Mc Guigan, I don't know him, but he was shot... blood... his face... he was murdered too, you know. And then, when I got over, you know the wee house... through the house, the far end. I went in and, you know, the pullover, they took it off me you see, they ripped it off up there... Did you see the wounds? You want to see them? Just stay... I was lucky there... just near the heart...

I tell you what happened then, after that. Did you see an ambulance? They took me over. There was one body there, dead, in the middle of the floor. He was dead, definite. I don't know the man's name, but he was dead, on the ambulance. He was dead, in the middle of the floor, I knew it. And there was another fellow sitting beside me, just like that, see, the way I'm sitting up now. As far as I am concerned, he was just leaning like that, there, and just a bullet wound here, through the head there, I thought he was not too bad anyway. In the corner where I was too... He was dead. And he was laying against me, like that. And there was the woman, what do you call her, Margaret

Deery, she was getting... she was pumping... And the Army was there galore... waiting just like that, you know, they would pounce at you right away. One word, you were still going to get the worst. The police and all was there, oh aye, the spite... they'd club you right away.

They would have clamped down on me right away if they knew that I'd said anything. We just had to walk out, no one came in to look for me... no doctor, no, no one, no one... Carried them out just like... you know... Only them people was there, we would have been dead. The hospital wasn't going to worry about us. Although there were people there, priest and all. They wouldn't let you see a priest... or nothin'. That's the Army... you see, the Army and the police and all.

Sure, Eddie (son), tell the truth... He went down looking for his brothers. He and the other boy. Charlie (son), the boxer, they went over...

Eddie: We went down to the morgue, and couldn't find him. We went back up to him (father) and told him and he says "No, Willy is dead... Willy is dead... I know he is dead, go and get him." So we went back down again and I went in again and said "I'm here to get my brother". He says: "You can't get anybody out here", he says. And I say: "I'm down here to identify him." And he says: "Right. Who are you?" And I says "Nash", I says: "William Nash, I'm down to identify William Nash." And he turns round and he says: "We've no call for you." "That's my right. I want to see him." And I went over and they brought me in and we walked in. And the place was crawling with police. There were four police men inside the morgue, not counting the detectives. And one turned and had an SMG, a Sterling sub-machine gun, and I went over... I'd seen my brother sitting... laying there... There were bodies all over... they didn't even bother to clean up the blood... they were just laying there. And I'd seen the way he was trailed, because I saw his face was torn.

They pulled the sheet down from the top of him. And I says: "That's him..."

And a wee detective... he was sitting and smiling away... And I spat at him, at the side of Willy's head... and I used language that nobody would be able to print... And I turned round and walked out on them all... and a wee stout fellow followed with a Sterling... he walked on to Charlie... Charlie spat at him... he pushed him... Charlie laid him across the floor... and then, as he went across, he turned around and would turn his Sterling around. And we followed McLaughlin, he came on then and pulled me out. I says: "I'm alright" and I get a hold of Charlie and pull him out.

But that's the way, they were laying like animals. In a slaughter house, in a slaughter house they take better care of the animals they butcher... in a slaughter house. What they did to them bodies. And they were human beings. Supposed to be, anyway. They treated them like animals down there...

Father: And he went down for his clothes, takes some telling. You know what he said, the policeman? Eddie, isn't it the truth? (Stuttering) Well, the policeman said (loud and clear): "One more Nash we haven't to worry about." Now, that's the truth... that's the truth. But they'll deny... they'll deny everything. You know what I mean, lying, all the time, lying. That's what's wrong. You see, Creggan Estate, or the Bogside? They'll never walk in it. You make no mistake about it, they'll never walk in this town.

LETTER TO JAMES AND SARAH WRAY,
AFTER THE MURDER OF THEIR SON JIM.

Loughgall
Co. Armagh
1st February 1972

Dear Mr and Mrs Wray (James and Sarah),

As I hold no regrets whatsoever for the death of your son James there doesn't be so much talk or fuss when some of the poor soldiers or policemen are brutally murdered in cold blood by the so called "Irish Rats Association". Yes, the "I.R.A." are the cowards, as your son was not shot by a cowards bullet, and he was not murdered, he was happily killed because he was a terrorist along with his other twelve Rebel friends.

Also remember that our troops are not serving on foreign grounds, Northern Ireland is part of the "United Kingdom", so the army is at home on British Territory. If you don't like living in this country, why don't you then move south or west to the bloody Free State? There we wouldn't have to pay you out our welfare benefits and allowances which you are gladly accepting under "Her Majesty The Queen".

"May sweet Jesus have mercy on his soul", ha! ha! what a laugh, that's what it says at your son's death in the "Irish News", what you should have stated is this "May Hell Roast Him" and the rest of his mates.

Your son was a fucking bastard and a fenian cunt, he was full of hatred so he can say goodbye to glory. Your Rebel bastards are doomed.

"The Wray family", get out of your home or be burned out.
Ulster is British, God Save the Queen. No Surrender.

Your enemies
Loughgall Head of "UVF"

So many other countries. As soon as they had a wee bit of an argument, they'd shoot them. They talk about the Russians, going into Hungary and all them places. They shot them people down, didn't they? We didn't shoot ourselves down. What about the young fellow that was shot at the Bogside last night? He had a drink. He was going home. We don't know who's doing this shooting from the Walls. You don't know it. Another dead. Them boys are being let loose with the rifles. We don't know who is doing the shooting from the Walls. It could be them boys coming along, getting a beer, taking a pot-shot, taking the rifle of a soldier and taking a pot-shot. See them soldiers? They give 'em beer. See that Sunday, when all that killing was going on, they brought them beer to the hospital. For the soldiers. Crates of beer. And it's happened in that hospital, and they allowed it. But we wouldn't get none of it. And TV and all got into it. And it's supposed to be the hospital, that belongs to the Derry people. They put them into the tearoom (the soldiers), with TV and all, I could walk around in that tearoom and watch TV at night, when I was alright. But I couldn't. Where was the TV? For the soldiers. They brought them crates of beer and great Irish drinks, and lit bonfires on Irish dead... for them. That's the truth.

Eddie: We checked out what Willy had. He had thirty pounds in his pocket when he went out, and we allowed him to spend three pounds ten for the dance. And it was ten shillings for the dance, and we allowed him the money for how many people he was taking. And it was three pounds ten. He had a chain and a cross. He had a gold graduation ring on his finger. When I went down to pick up his personal belongings, they handed me a comb and two bob... a ten pence piece... I wouldn't even go out with ten pence in my pocket, and I'm married.

A young fellow lost more than that. He had bar money. Ten pounds, maybe twenty pounds. There was nothing they had got. Everything was stolen. And then, see their clothes...

Father: ... See their clothes. That wasn't got yet. Even had a new suit, hadn't he, had new boots. None of that was got yet. You know what's going to happen? No one nearly checks them. The same with me. They didn't check me, but they had my clothes in hospital, they took my clothes off me too. They could do anything with them clothes. They could say, right, he was firing a nailbomb or something, a petrol, they threw petrol on me. They can put anything on them clothes...

Voice: (to small boy): What happened to your arm, (arm is in a sling)...

Small boy: It was shot. I just... I was walking behind the bread van. I was with my father, delivering bread. I walked out behind the bread van, in Eastway. I walked out behind the bread van and heard a shot... and it hit me. There was no rioting going on. They were shooting, just. I was going to a house to see how much bread they wanted. It went into the shoulder and stayed there. They had to operate me. I just turned round and says I was shot... I walked off with my father. I walked off there (laughs). We went into a house and he phoned the ambulance.

Voice: How old are you?

Small boy: Fifteen. Fourteen now and fifteen next month.

<u>In the house of James Joseph Wray, 22 years, murdered.</u>

Mother: I would love to ask Faulkner. He say's he's out to put the IRA down. How can he do it? It's the greatest advertisement for the IRA that we ever had. For when they go in and lift or kill somebody in the area, out of a family, what are the sons or relatives going to do? What are my boys going to do now? Are they going to sit back after their brother has been murdered? He has cousins, he has relatives, they have all the one thing: a hatred against the British Army and Faulkner. He's the best advertisement for the IRA and I would say he was their instigation in the North...

Father: Do you see, that idea that was put around the first days, and a lot of our people fell for it... They stated that the British Army on Bloody Sunday shot two men, hoping that the word would get to Creggan and bring these fellows down. The British Army didn't do that. The British Army had no intention... they knew the IRA were in Creggan and they wanted them there. Because if the British Army had thought that the IRA were on the ground, they wouldn't have moved in. Because it has been proved here, when the IRA was born out of necessity in this area, when we barricaded the area, and all we had was stone force, to keep the British Army out, on certain nights when they attacked the area, it was with one purpose in mind: just to drag men and boys off for internment and to brutalise them. Well, the stone throwers couldn't stop them from coming into the area, and the IRA banded together and fired a few shots. That kept the British out. That's when the IRA were born out of necessity. The people in the area... they are the only salvation that the people in the area have, they are the only weapon to keep the Army out... Well, now, the British Army, we have seen them on different occasions getting out of the IRA's way as soon as the IRA opened fire on them. Do you think that that same force that has retreated steadily for two years... if they had had a thought that there was an IRA man there they wouldn't have come on. They wanted to massacre unarmed civilians, that's what they wanted to do. Unarmed people were a threat to them. In 1968, when the Civil Rights Movement posed the greatest threat to them, with the people in the streets and Stormont said "Get the people off the streets, the rest of the world will not know it", they used the brutality that was acceptable in the North of Ireland at that time: they split their heads open with batons and what not... So, this time when the people were coming on the streets again, the British Government used what would be accepted in England, and that was a massacre of the people with the excuse of the IRA...

There is one thing that will bring it home to the English. That's when trouble starts in England and they can't say "All the trouble is in Ireland, let our boys over there carry on and battle them into the ground". When it comes to their own ground and trouble starts there, they'll say "Wash your hands of this". They should have opened a campaign, a strong campaign in England. We should pick a way to suit ourselves. But in Dublin they don't want to know. When these thirteen people died and they were talking about the burial, I said that I would like the thirteen coffins to go to Dublin, and come back again. For the way I had looked at it was this: you get an observer and he comes to Derry on Bloody Sunday and he goes to Dublin, which is over a hundred miles away, maybe a week afterwards, and he tries to tell a crowd what happened.

Well, you can't convey, like, what you saw. I saw blood running in the street, or I saw this or that... If the people saw the blood in the street, they'd get the message. That's why, to my mind, they should have sent the coffins and showed them in the streets...

People get on to the wife and me and say, like... they seem to think that we got over this bereavement very quickly... I take, and the wife takes consolation on knowing that he was murdered, that he was unarmed and he was brutalised and brutally murdered by British Paratroopers, cowardly Paratroopers.

And, like, I have a great sense of satisfaction on knowing that I reared a son... I am not trying to make him above anybody else, but... he was a noble boy. AND I WOULD SOONER HAVE FATHERED A BOY THAT WAS BRUTALLY MURDERED. I WOULD HATE TO BE THE FATHER OF A COWARD WHO HAD MURDERED HIM.

I hate to think to be the father of a coward who had murdered him. Like, he's not alone, there is lots of young fellows that are noble and are out fighting the British Troops.

I, my wife, my sons, my son Jim, who was 22, my son Liam, 19, my son Alec, 16, and my daughter Geraldine at 14, we went to Creggan where a Civil Rights march was taking place. We joined the group and we marched about three mile about the town, very good-natured, singing, laughing and talking. We were anticipating a bit of trouble from the Army, we thought they would fire gas at us. And I'd explained to my family before we left, we were to stay in a line on the streets, all together. I explained to them that the Army tactics would be to throw gas into the crowd, split them up and then come on and brutalise them. I told them that if they

Jim got a piece of tin... and two or three other fellows got the same...

were under an attack of gas, to try and keep together and make for a side street and get out of the main street, to escape imprisonment.

We arrived at the barricade at William Street and I'd say we were about a thousand and we knew the parade had been stopped. We went to the front of the barricade to see what was happening and we saw a few youths throw stones at soldiers. The Army immediately opened up with rubber bullets, gas and dye. And in the jammed streets that caused a great panic and pandemonium. I rushed for a side street, that was Chamberlain Street, and when I had recovered from this fit of coughing, I couldn't find any member of my family. I searched around, I got Alec who is 16, and Geraldine at 14, and told them to make their way home. I looked around for the rest of them and I saw Jim, sitting on his own, in front of the barricade... he had his beret on him, covering his head, and he had a handkerchief around his face up to his eyes, to prevent him from inhaling gas, and the Army were throwing gas and he was, with his hands signalling: "More gas! More rubber bullets!" Just in complete defiance of the British Army. He hated the British Army and what they stood for, and he was showing his defiance of them.

I went on, after the gas, and had a fit of vomitin' and coughin', and when I came back I couldn't see Jim. At this time the boys had been lifting up stones, boys and young men, they were trying to knock down a brick wall about five foot high, to try and get stones to throw at the Army. I couldn't see Jim, I walked up the street and I looked across "Aggro Street" at the other Army barricade, and there were two boys standing with the Civil Rights banner. One was Jim. I don't know who the other boy was. They were standing defying the Army again, just the two of them in the street. So, I went across to them, and at that, a bunch of fellows came... I don't know when Jim left the banner. But the boys started stonin' the British troops at the barricade. They fired rubber bullets and gas as we appeared, so stones were thrown at them. And Jim got a piece of tin, about three feet high, and two or three other fellows got the same and they were in the very front row. And their idea was: we trap the gas and rubber bullets and protect the boys who are throwin' the stones.

The Army got stoned for about ten minutes. A rubber bullet was fired in William Street and I dived down to get the rubber bullet. And it must have been as I dived down to get that rubber bullet, that the Army broke through. Because, as I got up William Street again, the first thing I saw was the Saracens crossing William Street. And I dived around the corner and made for Eden Place. I looked around as I was divin' and I saw Jim standing at the edge, where the old Rossville Hall used to be on the roadway. He'd seen and heard the Saracens and he didn't want to be ran over by them, so he stood and let three Saracens pass. And as the Saracens passed him, Jim moved out and ran up Rossville Street, with his hand in the air, throwin' a stone at the Saracens as they passed. That was the last time I saw Jim...

I made for Eden Place, one of the Saracens had turned after the left, to cut off Eden Place. I saw about five soldiers. I was the last off Eden Place, and as I got there the soldier was just at my heels... one of the paratroopers. There was a man standing there. He'd been overcome previously, to my mind. He didn't even know the Saracens were in the area. And this soldier pulled him around from a corner, and dragged him into the waste ground.

There were five or six fellows still in Eden Place, in front of me, and I said: "For God sake, give us a hand, don't let this man be arrested." At that time I thought he'd get his head split open. I didn't know the Army were opening fire. So, as I turned round, a half brick passed me and it took the helmet completely off the soldier. He immediately lifted his rifle and I turned to run into Chamberlain Street. I heard the shot and I saw the brickwork splatter above my head, and I dived around the corner into Chamberlain Street and I shouted: "They're shooting live ammunition." I looked back, along the further end of Chamberlain Street, towards the William Street direction, and there must have about a couple of hundred people runnin'

...there were two boys standing with the Civil Rights banner... One was Jim.

towards me. And I said: "For God sake get out, it's live ammunition." A couple of lads shouted it's only blanks. So, I was frightened and I ran straight across and I got into the back of the flats. When I got into the back of the flats, there is a small wall on the left, and I saw people cowering behind it. I saw a body outstretched and a priest kneeling over this person's head. I knew he wasn't a member of my family, but I wanted to try and identify him, in case somebody asked who was shot, so I crawled on my hunkers towards the priest. I was about three yards off him when I heard a person shout: "Shoot me, Shoot me... " I had never seen this person in the courtyard. It was a fellow with his hands above his head and he was shoutin': "Shoot me, Shoot me" and as I looked towards the flats, a soldier with his face blackened brought his rifle around to bear upon this man, and he opened fire. This man, I could see, was shot in the hip. I heard three shots bein' fired. I was more frightened then. I forgot about identifying this body. I didn't even attempt to help Bridges. My main thought was: get to safety. So I tried to get behind the wall, and as I glanced towards Bridges, there was a crowd coming from Chamberlain Street and they surrounded him to help him. And as I got to the wall to cover for safety, some people had jumped up from it and in the confusion we were all pushed around the corner of the flats and two more shots passed above my head. And I saw a person, at the wooden doorway, above the telephone box. People were saying he had a heart attack. I couldn't see any injuries on him.

To me he was dead, but I discovered later that this man hadn't died. I don't know what injuries he sustained. But I left and went across, to a sort of gangway with two small walls about three feet high. There was nothin' between that and Derry Walls. People were just cowering and crawling along this alleyway in case the soldiers opened fire from the walls. So we got to the foot of Fahan Street and I heard that people stood and told people: "Take a chance, now it's the time to run over." I couldn't assess it, but everybody was saying: "Now, take a chance... " And we got a lot of people back at Columbs Wells. Well, I went to my home, here, and I discovered that the only member of the family who hadn't returned home was Jim.

So, I went straight out and went back on the same way again. And, in my opinion, Barney McGuigan had been killed. I went to a priest and I asked how many bodies there were, that I heard that my son had been killed. I'd seen about five bodies at this time. My idea was, if he tells me there are six dead, that the other one would be Jim. He told me that, to the best of his knowledge, there were ten dead, on the ground, and he said there are three bodies in that Saracen, "but do not go near it because the Army would not let anybody to identify the bodies." So I came back home and about fifteen minutes afterwards the Knights of Malta came and told me... that my son's body... was in the morgue.

Mother: Before the march started he was sitting there and he was playing the record "The men behind the wire". And he kept playin' it and playin' it. And I come in (voice trembles all the time, slightly) and he said: "Mummy, I have a funny feelin', in my stomach...". And I says: "Maybe you ate your dinner too quick." He says: "No, it's not that, I've a feelin', I can't describe it." And I said: "Jim, maybe it's with the march startin', you're afraid there is going to be trouble." And he says: "No... I'm not frightened."

And I said to him: "If you feel like that, don't be goin' out." And he says: "Nobody will keep me in... from this march today." He says: "It's for them men, he says, that are in concentration camps." He says: "We have to free them... and it's a peaceful march..." So, we left the house... and Jim was always the first out, but he went down to the kitchen. And the father came back in and he says: "Jim, hurry up or we'll be late." And I went in, back to the kitchen, to him, and I says: " Come on, don't be standin' lookin' around the kitchen." He says: "I'm goin' now" and he came out the door, along with me.

We walked to Creggan. We were all together and he... he was so tall, he took big strides and I couldn't keep up and I said to him: "Jim, you'll be killin' me, you may slow up," and he says: "Mummy you'll be keepin' up easily." And when we got to the Bishop's Fields, they went over the wall and got on to the March and a man helped me over. Well, I was a bit behind, but then I got into line with them. And there were two of his friends, from his old home in Bishop Street and his father Jim, Alec, Geraldine and I. And I gave 'em cigarettes.

And he had his hat on, one which I knitted, and he had it outside in and jokingly I said to him: "Jim you're goin' to die with your hat outside in, they'll see all the knots in it."

And he laughed and says: "Why worry?" And... that's the last words... my son spoke...

When I got around Westland street, I fell behind, I couldn't keep up with 'em. I continued in the March and I got as far in William Street as the Fish Shop, when the gas got so bad, I had to go over the back entry. I looked around and I couldn't see any of 'em. And there was a girl standin' and she was soaked in dye, her clothes were soaked through. And she was tremblin' and we were all overcome with gas and I said to her: "Come with me and I'll get you a change of clothin'." And she said: "I've lost a friend, I'm worried about her, I fell." And I says: "Well, we'll look for your friend." So we went about, looking for her friend, couldn't get any, couldn't get her. And I says: "You'll have to come on home and get changed, or you'll be gettin' a cold." And I brought the girl across Rossville Street. A photographer took her photo as I was bringing her across. I got, up into the house. I got a hot bath goin'. Got her a change of clothin'. Took her own clothin' off her. Came down the stairs to make the girl a cup o' tea, when everybody seemed to fly around the back and round the street, screamin'.

And I opened the door and I called at the people: "Come in everybody, come in here." And a lot of people came in, I'd say there was about sixty people came into my home, and there were young boys and they said they were terrified, they were nearly shocked. There were young girls screamin' that they lost their brothers and their sisters.

So, I started and made tea for everybody. And we were three of us and we were makin' tea. And the father came in and it never caused me a thought. The son-in-law came in, he was soaked with dye. Then my other son came in and Alec came in, Geraldine came in and she started to cry. She was callin', she thought him... was dead. And I said: "Geraldine, that's nonsense. They wouldn't use live ammunition." And there was a little girl in here, and she started screamin' then, when she heard that they were shootin'. So, there was another wee girl, and she started to help me although she was scared, and started giving out the tea. She was one of the wee McKinneys, her brother was killed too... in Glenfada Park. And I didn't... I went out to the kitchen and the father said to me: "I've to prepare you, think Jim's arrested." And the words that I used to him: "I'd rather he was dead and he was carried in to me, than that the British Troops would get their hands on him, because they would only torture him... imprison him," and I says: "Prison is bad, but it's the beatings and torture and degrading that they do of 'em before they get in prison." And he says: "Do you mean that?" And I says: "Yes, I mean it. I'd rather Jim is carried in dead to me, than arrested by the British Forces."

So he called me up the stairs and as I went two girls came in to tell me, no, that it was only a rumour, that Jim wasn't dead. And I asked them what made them say that and they said they'd seen Jim standing down the street. And he was delighted, thinking Jim was living, but I turned to him then and I said: "No, Jim is dead." Because if Jim had been two doors down the street, he would have come in to let us know he was all right. And if they said they'd seen him there, my Jim... is dead, and that's... And I sent... When they went to identify him, I sent to the undertaker to seek to get his body out of the morgue immediately. And the undertaker said he couldn't get him out (voice trembles, almost breaks, but she carries on with great effort). But if he could get him out that night, he would do it for me. And I says I didn't want his body in that morgue (voice rises, still trembles). I said that they would tamper with their bodies and put things on them. And that was... the whole night long I kept on wanting his body out of the morgue. And in the morning I made him go at 9 o'clock, to phone to see could he get his body out.

And the only thing I'm sorry for (voice turns into a cry, all trembling gone) that the house he was in, in Glenfada Park... I know they have done their best for him... but I'm sorry they sent his body... to the morgue. I wish they'd brought him to his own home. And I don't care about inquest or anything. I am sorry my son lay in that morgue... for a night and a day... But I don't know what they'd done, for I couldn't see them, policemen in the morgue, and soldiers, respecting the dead... when they wouldn't let the priest do it, to give him the last rites of his church.

THEY LET MY SON DIE LIKE A DOG IN THE STREET, AND IF A PARATROOPER WAS LAYIN' DYING THERE NOW, I WOULD GO TO HIM AND SEE COULD I DO SOMETHIN' FOR HIM, AND I WOULD BRING HIS CLERGY TO GIVE HIM THE LAST RITES OF HIS CHURCH.

And I don't begrudge my son to Ireland. I don't. Because he stood against the oppression of the Irish people. And would he have come home on Bloody Sunday and if he would have found out 13 people was dead, he would have wished that he was one of them.

He was unarmed, when he was murdered.

ON THE SCENE

1st Boy: You know, there was a woman living in the house and she heard, and he, the commander, was standing outside the door and he was shouting: "Thirty is the limit." Ah, yes, did you hear about that too, we were up near the Walls and this para wrote: "The Paras were here, we'll kick the fuck out of you, you bastards" and then he wrote: "One Para – six coffins", on a plank on the wall. Then he came back and broke the plank and took it with him. It was just a short time ago, just after the shooting. We've never seen brutality like that, so he took it with him.

We saw two soldiers having a row because the Paras would be drawing out and they'd be left in. They're going to be the bunch that will be left in now, the Paras are drawing out, so they'll get the hammering.

You got the tape recording of the woman screaming and all. They were trying to shut her up and all. You got the best of the photographs and all the recording. We all heard it on the radio.

We were stuck up in that corner waiting to get lifted or shot. Yous were lucky you weren't killed. They were standing in the doorway with the SLR, across the road. Then one shot that girl in the leg (yous saw about the best of the action that went on down there), and we dragged the girl round the corner. Then his mate came round the corner to grab her. Then they opened up on us. We were caught IN THE CROSSFIRE FROM THE WALLS there, you know the City Walls. THEY WERE SHOOTING FROM THE WALLS. THEY FIRED THE FIRST SHOTS UP THERE, TO GIVE THE PARAS AN EXCUSE. I was fully caught in the crossfire. That's when they say they were opened up on. The Army says there was a carbine at the back of the flats, there was no carbine down there. The only people who have carbines are the Provos and there were no Provos down there, they were all up in Creggan. They came down afterwards. I know because they were asking what had happened. There was an agreement that no arms would be brought down on the day of the march at all.

You were nearly shot. You must have cracked up. or something, when you went out and started screaming at them. They fired three times at you.

We were sitting against the wall, there was a fellow sitting shouting his leg was broken. Somebody said, "Keep your broken leg, we're not moving out to get shot. You move over here." That's bad, you know. There was a guy shot in the head too.

Then I was hiding at the telephone box on the corner of the Flats. There were about 15 of us there. But, did you see that, that guy that opened up on you? You didn't see them. He was standing behind a Saracen. He was laying over the bonnet of a Saracen firing at the window.

You didn't see the old man lying on the barricade. He got shot, he raised his arm to get up again and the boy shot him again, in the head.

They blew the leg outta that girl, she'll never walk again. She was the first one I think. I dunno, aye, she was the first. You see, I was standing beside her, she stood in the corner, your man levelled an SLR. There was a wee hole in the front of the leg and the whole back of the leg was blown to ribbons. I lifted her legs and the boy lifted her head and the fat just rolled the whole way outta her. I was hanging on to her. They wanted to lift her. A soldier put his head round the corner and grabbed the woman and he had a rifle in his hand, so I gave it to him. I had a pole. He let go.

The troops over at Abbey Street had a Sterling and they got hit by a rock.

There were three of them standing on a corner and they were going to open up with a Sterling at a boy. He threw a stone and hit one on the head. If he hadn't done that he would have been dead. There were three boys shot there.

Seamus, the boy behind my friend, you see they ran past a Saracen and came out round the corner and a boy jumped out from the Saracen with a Sterling and started firing. If he hadn't fired his whole magazine so quick a whole lot of others would have got it. He pumped the magazine off against a wall. This boy was holding on to my clothes and then he dropped and I thought he had fallen and said "Come on" and then I turned. Jesus, he was dead. Shot in the back.

Another boy: There was a fellow shouting for help from the barricade, on top of the bodies. A man stepped out with his hands on top of his head and was shot in the stomach. He wasn't dead, he was wounded. There were three young lads lying face down, dead. There was a priest standing near us, he wanted to go out to help but we wouldn't let him go out. Just at that moment someone said the Army was coming, put your hands on top of your head and hope for the best. A soldier came towards the priest, just grabbed him, reached for him and his glasses came off. They have just told barefaced lies. It's terrible.

Another boy: Just a mass execution, that's all.

Fourth boy: You should see a girl who was round my house, she's been shot twice by the Army, in the stomach, just listen to her, she's still there.

Another boy: I saw young Wray getting shot, he was wounded in the arm and had blood above his right eye. I went running out to help him. He looked towards me in the house. I ran towards him to lift him up, then I heard shots fired and went running back into the house. I heard that man dying for the next ten minutes and saw him shot again, in the back at close range, I saw his coat jumping up and shortly after the paratroopers were behind him. I saw another young fellow across at the house waving a white handkerchief. When he cleared the corner he shouted: "Don't shoot" and he fell on the ground. And he had never moved at anyone. They were unarmed, everyone was unarmed. The soldiers were firing at everyone, they were firing at everyone from the Walls.

As a matter of fact, 20 minutes before the paratroopers came in they shot dead a couple of fellows in William Street. The Army fired a high velocity bullet across from between Sackville Street and Stevenson's bakery and I know an Army bullet when I see one. It's British Army bullets. It's embedded in the walls in a certain part of the Flats. I could show you all the bullet holes.

I saw soldiers that were firing indiscriminately. I saw six shots fired into the crowd. Four shots unaimed. I saw another fellow fire two shots. I saw three aimed shots from two paratroopers towards the high grass bank near the Walls. I saw a paratrooper kicking people as they marched them off and I didn't know there were three men shot dead, behind this man Wray, who was shot dead. Jesus, Jesus, I didn't know there were three more men shot dead 10 or 12 yards round the corner and one of the men carried in had three bullet wounds in him, that also proves he was shot while he was lying on the ground wounded. There is no man that could stand up if he was hit by a SLR bullet in the body.

Man: I know what I'm talking about. I've had 18 years Army service and I know about weapons because I've taken part in shooting competitions. I also know that the paratroopers know their job because their rifles were tuned down to allow the minimum amount of noise when they pressed the triggers.

Boy: I heard this man Wray for about 10-15 minutes as he lay on the ground. He had a cut above his left eye and his right arm was injured and I understood, I was nearly sure he was shot in the arm from some place, I heard him for a long time, he lay there, his head was down, he got unconscious, and I told the people in the house that he was wounded. They said it was a soldier. I said no, it wasn't a soldier because I saw a paratrooper circling around him and he didn't bother to pick him up. If it had been a soldier he would have lifted him and brought him off. I saw a second paratrooper coming shortly after that. I saw the man's jacket leap up into the air about four or five inches twice, I told the people in the house that the man had been shot again in the back, twice at close range. I saw what I thought was smoke as the bullet hit his body. I then saw the paratrooper stepping forward about four or five yards beyond where this man was lying dead and later I discovered that there were three men lying dead behind that man and one was shot three times.

I witnessed this man dying or dead. I even know where the bullet wounds were, as I pulled up the man's coat. There were two bullets in his back, one on his left side came out his right shoulder blade, one in his right side.

My parents live in England, my brothers and sisters, father and mother. I'll never go back to England again.

Voice: Good for you. Cold-blooded murderers.

Voice: If you want to murder anyone, cold-blooded murder, and get away with it, join the British Paratroopers.

Another boy: We were next to Father Murphy, with the ambulance just at the front of the Flats, the Rossville Flats. If that ambulance had moved off we would have been dead, they were shooting at everything that moved. It was just like a shooting gallery. They say in the News that there was sniper fire, that was ridiculous. There was no sniper fire at all.

The shooting then stopped. I left with Father Murphy, he came out waving a hankie from behind the ambulance, and they stopped then. That's how I got out, behind the ambulance, with Father Murphy and a couple of other blokes. Only that, as I said before, if the ambulance had moved off we'd have been dead because they were shooting at the ambulance too.

Another boy: Also the army put out, just now in the News, that there were men armed. These so called armed men were shot in a crowd. Nobody ran out for them. There were two men that were gunned down in cold blood from a Saracen. They were murdered. They were gunned down from an armoured car. No one ran out for them. Therefore the Army were the first to reach them. The Army never found guns on them or nail bombs.

Another boy: You see, there was about six boys near the Saracens, then there was two lifted. The Army were in good positions and could see another three lying dead. Then the Army came on the News and said there were only two dead. There were five lying dead, plus the four shot in Glenfada Park. If the IRA had been sitting in Glenfada Park the Army moved in so fast that everyone sitting there would have been shot dead.

But the statement the Army came out with is ridiculous. As you know there were no petrol bombs or nail bombs used. Then they say there was sniper fire, but there wasn't. It's all lies. It was them that were doing all the shooting.

I thought there were about 40 shot. The way the Army was going on, they seemed to be going berserk. In fact, more than 30 got shot, and 59 arrested.

The Army must have executed the boys that were already arrested. Mc Daid was arrested. He was seen on T.V. with some cameraman. They said he was arrested, put in the back of a Saracen, an armoured car, a gas canister was tossed in the back of the armoured car, he ran and they shot him.

There is an alleyway in the Bog. They said: " Come out with your hands up." About 20 boys came out and the last three out of the alley were shot in the legs as they walked across the road. Your man, he was only small, standing with a rifle and he shot them in the legs as they walked across the road. Can you imagine that?

About 20 boys went through a gap. I imagine to get away when the Saracens charged, and a soldier turned it (a rifle) on them and he shot a boy, one of my friends, in the back. He grabbed him, he didn't know he was dead. He pushed him off and he ran off.

How could there be 20,000 liars. How do we get 20,000 liars to tell the same story? Like, us people, we are all strangers to one another, like, we've got different ideas of God, we're liberals and moderates and socialists and all sorts. How do you get 20,000 odd people in the Bog to tell the same story that the soldiers opened fire on us? Are we all liars, 20,000 odd of us? How can we be liars? 20,000 plus one Italian journalist. I am glad that people like you exist.

BBC idiot came on to say that the most dramatic pictures were the ones on the news where the March began blah blah blah.

1st Girl: Before anything happened I was at the barricade at the bottom of Rossville Street. Then the organisers of the March asked everyone to assemble at Free Derry Corner and I moved up with the crowd. When I got to Free Derry Corner the platform was all set up for the speeches, for the speakers. The first to come was Bernadette Devlin and she had some talks with the people about the soldiers. Then we all stood around Bernadette and all of the other speakers all got on the platform. It all started then. Bernadette got up. She started her speech with: "The only rioters here today are the British Army" and not to pay any attention to them. So the people stood by and listened to the speakers. She just started her speech when the troops had moved to the bottom of the barricade. Everyone started to shout at the soldiers, then we all stood and sang. She didn't get saying much of her speech when everyone started to get onto the platform.

Me and my friend had just got on and we were standing behind Bernadette and other speakers when a canister of gas was thrown. We stood there when Bernadette said to the crowd we were to stand our ground because there were 15 of us to every one of them. This is before they opened up with their live rounds of ammunition. We stood on watching from the platform at the antics of the British Army. The boys stood by, none interfered with them.

Then everyone started squealing. There seemed to be shots coming from the bottom of the street. We all ducked down from the lorry. Bullets were ricochetting off the wall where it said Free Derry Corner.

The banner was shattered. Fellows jumped from the lorry. In fact I heard later two of the men who were holding the banner standing at the wall were shot dead.

Well, everyone panicked, the place was in a state of panic. I too jumped down from the van pulling my mate behind me. The first I met was an old woman of about 60 years of age. She stood up against the wall, scared to move. She thought if she moved she would have been shot dead. We tried to persuade her to move on, but she wouldn't. She was in a daze, scared of being shot dead. Her fingers were clawing the wall.

We all started running. I don't know if she was removed or not, but we all started running. I ran on ahead of my mate, I kept looking round for her but she kept trailing behind me. Then some elderly woman grabbed on to my coat and started squealing for me to wait for her. Then I fell over someone, then someone fell over me and I just jumped over the barricade. I don't know how I did it. I was over the barricade, the shots were flying everywhere. People were falling over everyone.

Then I saw a young girl crying and women were crying and people were everywhere. It was just a state of pandemonium.

The first thing I knew, my mate was behind me shouting for me to wait on her. She was shouting: "Liz, I can't run any further", so I went back for her, telling her if she didn't she would be shot dead.

Well, all this time bullets were just whizzing over our heads. It was a miracle we were saved, and I stood in the middle at the barricade. I just ran on and I didn't know the district and I stood in the middle of the courtyard and ran for somewhere to go but couldn't find anywhere, because I was a stranger to the district.

Then a woman who lived in the Bogside came over to me and said: "What are you standing there for?" and I said: "I've nowhere to run to" and she said: "Quick, over here", and she took me away.

Then the soldiers surrounded the square and they started shooting down the square. I began running again, then I met up with my mate. She had fallen and just then a bullet whizzed over her head. I started crying, I thought she was dead and I thought I was all alone in the courtyard.

Then some fellow was coming to her aid and I ran over. He bent down to pick her up. Then some shots rang out and he fell and she got up. She was limping, she had hurt her knee, that was all, but we didn't know what to do about the fellow. There was nothing you could do for him or you would be shot dead yourself.

Then I asked some fellow: "What way would we run?" and he said: "Run into this entry", and I ran and I came in front of a soldier and he shouted: "HALT", but I ran on, but this one, just this one, never opened up, he never shot any shots at all after me.

Me and my friend just ran and ran until we came to a house with the doors open and we ran in and that was the last we saw of that young fellow. We knew he was dead. The shooting had ceased a while when we came to this house. They brought us in, the people were very kind and gave us our tea.

Then this woman had gone out, onto the street, and got us a car to drive up to the Creggan Estate. We waited there for the rest of the people of the Belfast crowd to arrive and there again we were taken into someone's house and given something to eat and then taken away on a bus, down to Foyle Street, where our bus home was parked.

2nd girl: We had reached the end of the march, down the bottom of William Street where there were Saracens and water cannons right across the street. I couldn't see any soldiers and the people just stopped and I saw a couple of stones being thrown. There were only about two or three that I saw. There was no singing or chanting. The next thing I saw was a big jet of dirty black water flying around the people and gas canisters at the same time.

Then pandemonium broke out, people started to scream, women were screaming and you couldn't run to the left because you knew to the left the Army were manning the streets for about five streets up. You could only run to the right and there were no openings and you could only push those that were behind you, getting them to turn back and get away.

In the end I got behind an old building and I saw three first aiders there, their eyes were swollen with tear gas. I was trying not to be sick and at the same time I was choking. I tried to get my scarf tied round my mouth to protect me from the gas and everyone was squealing and we saw the first aiders trailing this man who had collapsed under the gas.

It eased up a bit after that and I stayed there until I got my breath back and then I started to make my way up toward the hill and when I got to the top of the hill, I hear someone with a microphone saying: "Make your way to Free Derry Corner, there will be a meeting at Free Derry Corner."

I asked someone where this was and he pointed it out. You went round this corner and then way up. I think it was Rossville Street but I knew when I arrived at it because it was written on the wall. There was a coal lorry there and as I got to it, so Bernadette Devlin arrived. She was called up onto the lorry as were other speakers that were available. We waited a few minutes and started to sing some song then.

Then another speaker arrived. He was a Lord and 83 years of age. And the two boys who had been heading the parade and carrying the banner arrived and we helped them onto the lorry.

After this someone said to the crowd: "Will you please make way, Ivan Cooper has come now." Ivan Cooper and another man climbed onto the lorry. Bernadette Devlin told the people to be calm and there was nothing to worry about. She said we out-numbered the British Army 15 to 1. There 3,000 troops, so that made us 25,000 people. That was when I realised how big it was. It was the largest protest march I had walked in and we stood and listened. Bernadette said: "I will introduce the first speaker" and that was Lord so-and-so, when bullets started flying all over the place.

She said for everyone to duck down as they had started shooting. The bullets were ricocheting off the walls, we all ducked and again a woman started squealing and running up towards what I would say was the Creggan way. I was always heading towards that way. I called to my mate Liz and her chum not to run with the crowd but to stay close to the wall, that was the safest part and to stay low, but Liz got carried on in the crowd and I got onto the wall and stayed there until the shooting stopped. Then I made my way up to the barricade. It was poles, stones and bars, and a man helped me across and he asked me if I was alright. He asked me on hearing my accent where I was from. When I told him Ardoyne, Belfast he said: "Then you'll know what it's all about, you are used to this." I said "Yes." I was.

I asked if I could help him. Then I saw another friend of mine in an archway and went over to him. Then we helped women as they came along, some were crying, some had blood on their dresses, some had no shoes, one had lost her handbag. They were all panic-stricken.

When there was another lull in the shooting I decided to go over to the other side to see if I could find my friend Liz and her chum, or another friend John who had come over from England for the March. I went across the street where there was a square with flats and I was going to ask a man with dark glasses who he was reporting for. He had a cine-camera with him, but then I saw some people standing against a wall, someone was buying lemonade, there was a shop there, so I went down there to get lemonade as my mouth was still burning after the gas.

As I came out there was more shooting. I ran to the wall where I saw other fellows running and I held tight to it as they did. I stayed there until there was another lull in the shootings. The fellows said: "Mrs, you had better make your way up the hill." I asked which way and enquired about my friend Liz and gave a description. They hadn't seen her, so I made my way up the hill when more shots rang out. So I ran out of the way. It was on Tuesday when I saw McKinney's photograph, that I realised he was the man I had spoken to. He was shot where I had been standing and where he was filming.

Another boy: I was in the March, in William Street. And when the March reached William Street I was in front and I tried to stop the crowd throwing stones. We didn't want any trouble. And they brought the watercannon up and we all ran and I ran into Chamberlain Street, when a soldier turned round the corner. This was when they moved down, soldier turned round the corner with a rubber bullet gun, and he fired it at me. And then I was standing with a stone... I was waiting for him to come round again, and the next that came round was a soldier with an SLR and he fired two or three shots above my head. And I called to the crowd that now they were shooting... and I ran up Chamberlain Street and I was just out into the square when Jackie Duddy... he was the fellow who was in front of me... he was shot... he got shot in the back and in the head and ... then I just ran... in the middle of the square... there was this other man, Mickey Bridge... they were shooting at the priest, and the priest was giving Jack Duddy the last rites... and Mickey Bridge started, you know, to shout: "Shoot me, don't be shooting at the priest"... and they shot Mickey Bridge in the leg... and I... you know... went into hysterics... cracked up and Harry knocked me out... and I was there for about ten minutes, until, you know, after the shooting.

And... as we were going around the corner, over the flats, we were walking over, and as we were going round, to the front... it was like something I had seen in a cowboy picture... there was no live person walking about, everybody... it was just bodies lying all over... and then... there was this girl friend and I carried her into a house and the minute I went into the house there was bodies lying all over the place in the house and I was going to fall apart... In Rossville Street. And that was when all the shooting finished, then. That was the last I heard.

Barney McGuigan, he was shot near the telephone box. Barney McGuigan was with us before he was shot. He says: "Come on round to the front of the flats... you'll be safer." And he crawled over, the wee wall. And the next thing when we went up round the front, there he was lying at the telephone box... dead. And Paddy Doherty too, from Hamilton Street, he was... lying opposite the door of the bakery. Well, he was shot dead. He was shot from the Derry Walls, I think.

I've seen Frankie, he was trying to give Gilmore the kiss of life... and the blood started coming up Gilmore's mouth and Frankie just walked on and said he couldn't do nothin'... And then he pulled Gilmore into the flats... That was all the deaths I've seen...

And then, about seven o'clock that night I went up to the house. My father thought I was shot, then my other brother was in. And then I says: "Where is Joe?" You know, that's my brother. And my father says: "I never heard nothin'" and the girl friend that was there told me that Joe was shot... You know I never believed her and then this man come over the house and he told us he was in the hospital and I says: "How bad is it?" and he says: "Well he's not too bad." He didn't want to say, you know, he was pretty bad, but he didn't want to say it.

And then my father went over to the hospital and then we heard he was shot in the chest... He was shot in Glenfada Park, he was along with John Wray and some other fellow and... the three of them were rounded up and the soldiers told them to stop and some of 'em put their hands in the air and I think they stopped then. The soldiers just mowed them down... And Jim Wray, he was shot dead. Jim Wray was lying there and the soldiers ran up and he moved his head and the minute he moved his head they shot him again.

But my brother when he was shot, he just kept on runnin'... He thought he was hit by a rubber bullet... until the blood started up his mouth and then he looked down and put his hand down... and the blood was coming out...

The priests tried to reach the Saracens, to give the last rites to the men that were on the Saracens, and the Army told them to get back, not to get near them, but a priest went up to the Saracen, made his way up to the Saracen. He saw three bodies in the Saracen... piled on top of one another. The man below... his tongue was swollen out of his head, of his mouth. He was wounded, but it wasn't from his wounds that he died, it was from lack of air, because his tongue was swollen up just out of his head.

This was about four o'clock. So, he immediately went to the hospital, to wait on the arrival, to give them the last rites. But he waited two hours. The bodies weren't brought in till six o'clock.

IN HOSPITAL

Danny McGowan, 32 years.

I was near the front of the flats, behind Joseph Place. When the shooting started I was there, I was looking for my wee fellow. I've got a brother-in-law who lives in St Columb's Walk. I was looking up at the suspension of his lorry, and I heard the shooting. And I darted up for my young fellow. He is fourteen. He is at the college, St Columb's College. Ran down to see where he was and I seen people running all over the place. A man came by... he was hit in the back. His name is Campbell. He is up in ward eight at the moment. And I tried to give help to Mr Campbell to get him out of the road. And I was hit in the leg, I fell... and two people dragged me away and took me in a taxi, or a car, I didn't know what it was. And we tried to get out (the man's voice gets shaky, he has obvious trouble in going through the visualisation again)... by Bishop's Street... the Army was there... there was a car in front of us... a couple of people hurt, and they shot rubber bullets at us. So the driver turned back, took me home, and my brother got me an ambulance, and I came out to the hospital, and they gave me an anaesthetic, and I fainted, and that's all I know. They never guarded me, this place. I was just brought here, and my leg fixed up. I also saw one, one young fellow lying at the shops. This was after I had been hit. I have seen him lying at the telephone box. And there was a girl, kneeling over him. He had a sweater on, no coat. I got hit three, four minutes after the shooting began. I think the shot came from the Walls. The position I was in, the bullet went in the left side of my leg, came out at my foot, the right side. There was no Saracen. It must have come from Derry Walls. I can't move my leg. Just my toes. The bone was shattered.

I'm a maintenance service man. I wasn't on the march. I was down, looking at the suspension, the suspension of my brother-in-law's lorry. He lives in St Columb's Walk, beside Free Derry Corner. The two people that dragged me away, they said the shots had come from Derry Walls, and shots were coming from Derry Walls at them. They had to get down and drag me, like that, along. The same person that dragged me away dragged Mr Campbell away, who's in Ward 8 upstairs. The same two people... He was shot in the stomach and the back. I was very much in pain as I was hit. I had to drag myself along the ground, maybe 15 or 20 yards, me leg was shattered... and the bone was sticking through my leg. And these two people came and helped me (seems moved)... thank God... very good people...

Damian Donaghy, 15 years.

I was in William Street when the shooting started, near the waste grounds, I was going over to my cousins in the flats. I was in William Street and was taking a short cut, you see. I wasn't in the march. Taking a short cut through the waste ground, heard the rubber bullets... and then heard a shot, and fell... and me leg... seen the blood. Shouted to a man I'd been shot. He came over, that man, and he was shot, when he was helping me. He got shot in the arm and in the leg. And I got carried in to a house, got no bandage... taken over here... priest (has difficulties in expressing himself, is still shattered)... I got carried away, into a house, by a crowd, near Glenfada Park, you know, near William Street.

The bullet hit the kneecap, broke the bone, came out below, behind the leg. I was the first hit, in William Street. Just a bit into the waste grounds, before the Saracens came in. They shot from the roof of the sorting Post Office.

I didn't feel the bullet. Then my leg was twisted. I thought it fell off (his voice breaks). Half-an-hour later I was taken away by a car. There weren't any ambulances. Wouldn't let them in. I had a cousin shot. Gerry Donaghy. He was shot dead.

I don't know how long I'll stay in here. Another ten weeks, I think.

I was brought into this woman's house. And I heard the Saracens moving in, heard all the shooting. I wasn't afraid, when I was in the house. Afraid when I was shot.

When the thing right happened. Then the crowd came and helped me. And a man was shot twice, in the arm and in the leg. He's called Johnston. That's all.

Michael Christopher Bradley, 22 years.

On that day, the Bloody Sunday, the 30th January, I was down in William Street. And when the battle started we were standing there for quite a long while. The first thing I noticed was CS gas. They attacked us. I automatically ran out of the road (remembering, he gets excited, shaken, his voice, although he tries to control it, trembles), though I was coughing and spluttering all over the place. Next thing I realise is the Army has sent in the watercannon which shot dye on everyone. People's clothes got ruined by the dye. I was lucky, I got out of the road. I stood there another five to ten minutes and I headed back towards William Street. Towards the back of the shop. It is a lane-way which takes you over to the Rossville area, to the High Flats.

On my way over the crowd started to come up behind us, they were running, and they were shouting: "Everyone run quick, here comes the Army... " I was half way across the waste ground, which was used to be known as Pilots Row, when all of a sudden I looked towards Rossville Street, at the junction with William Street, and I saw three Saracens coming across. They cut up Rossville Street and the cut through the waste ground... and towards us.

I had run into the square behind the flats, behind the High Flats. I had run into there... the Saracens coming after us (face is drawn, eyes shiny, voice hectic with a slight tremble, the posture is rigid)... I ran right through, out to the opening of Joseph Place. I stood there for a few seconds, to pause and catch my breath. Other people were coming through and were shouting at us: "Would yous move out of the road and let us through." I automatically moved out of the road.

Just at that someone shouted: "There's a young lad shot." His name was Jack Duddy. A personal friend of my own... a friend of my own. So, first thing that came to my mind was to try and go out and help. I ran out, ten or twenty yards from where I was standing, and I ran out towards him. But when I got there, there was a crowd before me, and in the centre... was the young lad's body... in a puddle of blood. So, first thing that came to my mind was... I was just mad with anger. Though I was carrying nothing at the time, I had neither brick, stone or nothin' in my hand, I turned round and I started using a lot of swearwords, bad language, at the soldiers.

Now, this time there was two Saracens in the square, at Rossville Street, facing me behind the High Flats. They were in the car park facing me. The soldiers had come out from inside their Saracens, taken up positions and firing points. Now I don't know which of these soldiers had shot me... Just at that moment everything was just... a flash... to me.

The bullet came through my left arm, into my chest, and out through my right arm. It wasn't until it came out from my right arm that I really knew I was shot. I called for mercy... I screamed... and I have seen the blood, running down my fingers. All of a sudden, I got up and ran towards Joseph's Place again, when four men grabbed hold of me. They took me to a nearby house... where I was laid out... ambulance men was sent for, like, first aid men. They came in, gave me attention...

A priest was brought in to me, and I was screaming for mercy... hoping... screaming for my life, like, you know... hoping that I wouldn't die. All around me, there was bullets flying everywhere...

Now, the only ones that I'd seen shooting that day was British soldiers. And as far as I'm concerned, I've seen that parade, I've seen everything about it. And I've seen stewards chasing men away from the parade, who wouldn't come into it peacefully. And as far as I'm concerned there wasn't a gunman in sight that day. Although I can't swear to this, but still I'd nearly give up my life for it. Which I already did.

When I was taken from the house to the ambulance, before that I laid in the house for what seemed to me three quarters of an hour. And I thought there was no one coming for me, and someone shouted there was the ambulance. The British soldiers wouldn't let the ambulance through at the start. But when they got through to me, I was taken on a stretcher, on wheels. The Army had opened fire upon us. Now, I didn't know this until I heard the crowd shouting... and waving white flags... "Don't shoot, this man is injured..." I was brought into an ambulance, there were three bodies put in beside me, and I looked down... I didn't know whether they were dead or not... But the young priest who saved my life, was chewing a bit of gum and he said to me, he says... I says: "Father, they are dead?" He says: "Yes"... He just blessed them there and then.

I was taken to hospital. And after that... everything was just blank to me. I couldn't mind anything for the next three days, like...

The ambulance was brought up Rossville Street, a few yards from the telephone box. I minded that distinctively, because, though I was shot I had full consciousness of what was going on. That is one good thing about it. Though I was screaming for mercy, I still minded everything that was going on. I don't know who shot me. But it was deliberate. They knew they were shooting at us and we were unarmed. They definitively... they must have known this, they must...

My left arm is broken. There is a clean hole cut through it. My chest, I have two holes in my chest, which I didn't realise I had. Because when people come into the hospital to visit me, I told them: "Oh no", I said "it's only a flesh wound." Until the second week, when the nurse was changing my dressing, I happened to look down and seen the holes. The two holes were about the size of a shilling piece. Although, at the time, I was very alarmed, and cried, like, because I had just seen these ones, because thinking... it was just a few inches away from my heart. Now, my left arm is shattered. I had to have a skin graft from my right leg, to cover this hole which is in my arm. My right hand, I can hardly move. At the moment it's useless to me, at the moment. The nurses here... are feeding me...

At the moment, I've to be fed by nurses... I have to be washed by nurses, shaved by nurses, have practically to be taken to the toilet by nurses. I can do nothing for myself. My right arm is killing me at the moment... it's so badly busted open... I'm a painter and decorator by trade, but at the moment, like, I was unemployed at the time.

They are trying to make it out here in the ward, some of the MPs and soldiers, that we weren't hit by British bullets. I'm afraid we were. Because the holes are distinctly... My mate in the ward, a doctor distinctly told him that he was hit by a high velocity bullet. So, I mean, there must be some proof, when even the surgeon knows what hit him...

You see that man over there, with the shattered leg, Mc Gowan. He had two uncles killed in Dunkirk, for Britain, a cousin in Salerno, his brother was in the British Army, three cousins in the Army, one was a sergeant major, another uncle killed in Monte Cassino...

Also, when we came into this hospital, we heard of rumours that that night, when the paratroopers had come back into the barracks, there was a massive row. Some of the soldiers here deny it, some of the MPs deny it. But one soldier told me that he had heard, I could give his name, but I won't unless I get him into trouble, he told me straight, he said that he heard there was a terrible fight that night and the paratroopers were told to get out, because after all the soldiers that were left would have to face the consequences.

A VISITOR

See, I remember at Magilligan, when we did that march to the internment camp. I mean, they say this, the paratroopers say that about Bloody Sunday, that they were fired on and all the rest of it. But when we were at Magilligan, we were only on a sandy strand, where there were neither stones, bullets or nothing else. But they still attacked us like cannibals, drawing batons and rifles also, and hitting us on the head and everywhere else. I myself got knocked on my head with a baton, which knocked me unconscious about two or three minutes. I was told afterwards, when I had recovered, that while I was on the ground they were kicking me and hitting me and everything else, like, you know. And I came over to hospital and I had four stitches in my head, and I was told to come back the next week, but when I came back the next week the stitches had come out, they'd never held, like. So I had to have it restitched again, and I was confined to hospital for a week...

Boy about 16

(Lays curled up, a tube in his stomach, in obvious strong pain. Seems still shattered. Speaks stuttering, trembling, face mostly buried in the pillow) I was... I heard a man was shot... I went down to the house where he was... In Colmcille Court. He was in a house there... there was about twenty of us... twenty of us, you know, standing at the door. And my man was in the house. And at this time... I remember... I went out to the flats... and we didn't know. I left then and I... I walked up to the maisonettes, up towards Glenfada... Glenfada Park. And as I was standing there, I saw these three boys lying shot at the barricade... and I went over, you know, to the row of houses, at the corner. And the shooting was going on, and I saw these three boys laying there, and I turned and walked away and saw this other boy... at the corner... the corner of the flats... and I kept walking and heard a bang... me leg gave way... I was lying there. After a while... I thought it was a rubber bullet... I could move me leg again... I was going to rise... and this one, he let on he was dead, he let on he was dead. They must have thought I was dead too, because they walked past me. That was the only reason that I wasn't arrested... For about ten minutes... among them soldiers. And I saw shooting... you know, shooting. And they went through. They arrested these boys that were trying to get back out of the house... I lay there watching, with one of me eyes open... watching... There was this woman coming on, and the woman stopped, and the boy kicked her twice in the stomach, with the butt of the rifle... and the paras came running down after a crowd of boys that were arrested... I asked to be taken into the house... I was safe for ten minutes. They got a car to take me to the hospital in a car. But the ambulance arrived... they took me over here in the ambulance. That's the last, the last I remember...

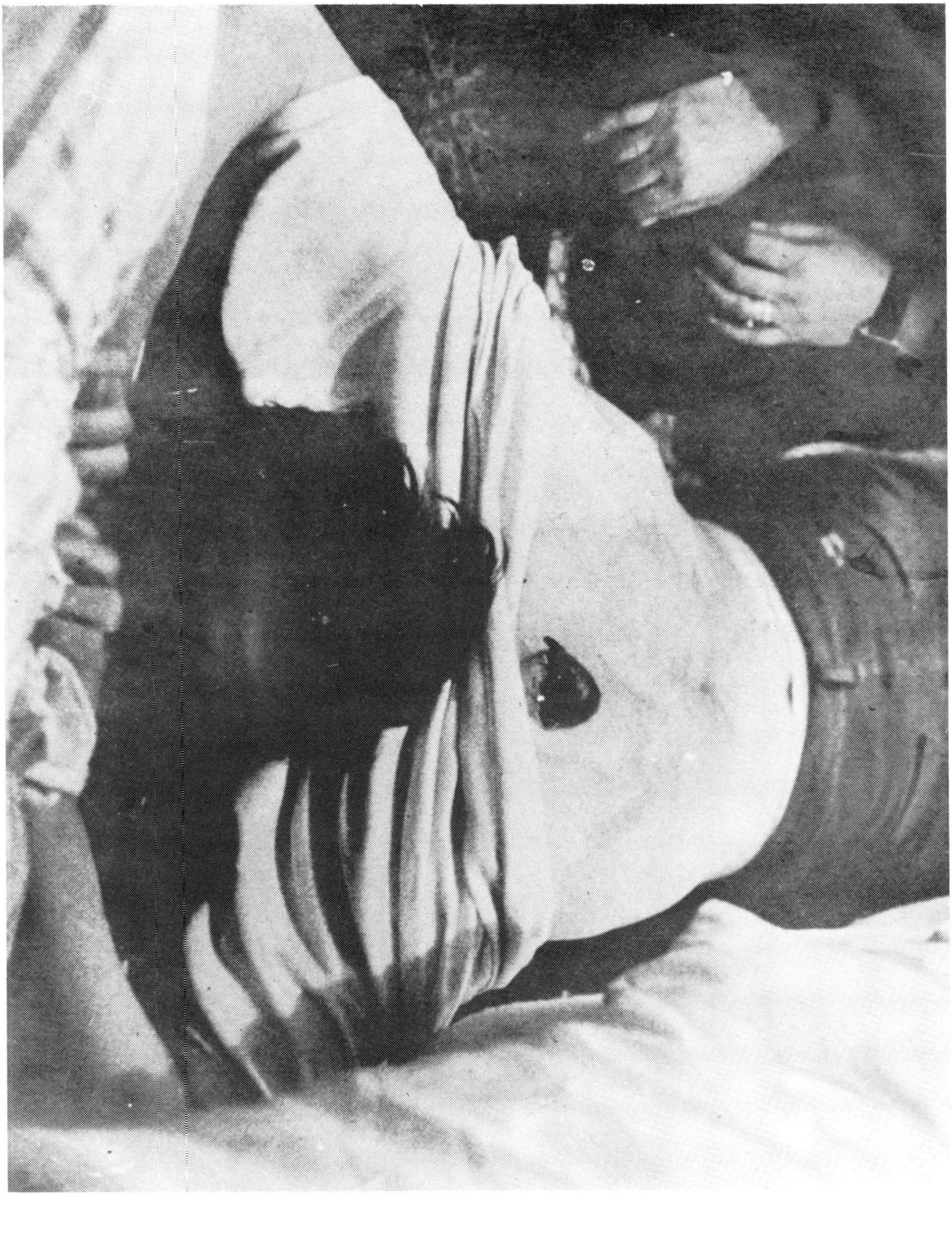

...chasing a boy with a handkerchief on his face; the boy falls;

...para-trooper steps over him... an arm raises, to shield, to plead;

fires — the mass jerks, lays still.

1st Bn The Parachute Regiment
Palace Barracks
HOLYWOOD, Co. Down
Northern Ireland

1 February 1972

Dear Wives,

Further news: The Battalion is now preparing itself for the inquiry from England which is to be held soon. 1 PARA will surely emerge from close scrutiny of the events of Sunday with colours flying honourably as usual. The wicked propaganda directed against us may well be turned to increase our professional reputation.

"D" Company have now returned to Palace Barracks, they are unlikely to have any specific task today or tomorrow. "C" Company spent all night sorting out the barricades in ANDERSONSTOWN. There was nil reaction as they successfully completed this operation.

The remainder of the Battalion are staying at "DERRY" until at least Wednesday evening. This is to cover any reaction from the BOGSIDE during the first of the funerals which is planned for tomorrow.

Reminder: Block leave is just two weeks away.

M V Stevens

M V STEVENS
Captain
O.C. Rear Party

Other titles available from

GUILDHALL PRESS

When the President Calls
Julian O'Neill & Trevor Birney

Perceptions – Cultures in Conflict
Adrian Kerr

The Making of a Minority – Political Developments in Derry and the North 1912-25
Colm Fox

No Go – A Photographic Record of Free Derry
Barney McMonagle

Country Roads – Walks on Foyleside and Inishowen
Sam Mitchell

Parade of Phantoms II
Peter Mc Cartney

The Wile Big Derry Phrasebook
Seamus McConnell

The Road to Bloody Sunday
Dr Raymond McClean

Thunder & Clatter – The History of Shipbuilding in Derry
Gerald Hasson

Brits Speak Out
John Lindsay